Alvin never found a place where he belonged, so he did what no one else would—he snuck into the Allegheny forest. He hoped to find a home there, but things are more complicated than he expected, so he's been roaming the forest, alone and starving, not knowing how to get himself out of this mess.

Then a coyote shifter bites him after he hears something he shouldn't have.

Roman is the new healer for the skunks, but he feels he has no idea what he's doing. At twenty-four, he was never supposed to have this role, and he's still grieving the death of his mentor.

When Roman hears whimpers coming from the forest one evening, he expects to find a wounded animal, not a half-starved human who shouldn't be there.

Roman can't keep Alvin's presence in his home a secret, but telling the council means they might kick Alvin out of the forest. Alvin might have been able to deal with that, but when he falls for Roman, he knows that whatever happens, his place is in the forest.

But some people disagree, including the surfeit's previous alpha, who is plotting his next steps from his cell in the council jail.

Not the Enemy
Copyright © 2024 Catherine Lievens
ISBN: 978-1-4874-4124-1
Cover art by Angela Waters

Published by eXtasy Books Inc

Look for us online at:
www.eXtasybooks.com

Not the Enemy
Allegheny Shifters 13

By

Catherine Lievens

CHAPTER ONE

It had been a long time since Roman had been excited to visit one of his patients. Since Janice had disappeared, he was always afraid he'd do something wrong and end up killing them instead of helping them. Having someone's life in his hands was terrifying. It always had been, but before, he'd had someone with experience working next to him, helping him and taking things in hand if he failed.

He couldn't afford to fail anymore.

At only twenty-four years old, he'd become the official skunk healer. No one else could do the job, and he couldn't abandon his people, no matter how shaky he felt. He'd always hoped he would become the skunk healer eventually, but he'd thought he'd have at least ten more years of training with Janice. She'd been in her sixties, so there should have been plenty of time for Roman to learn from her.

But Janice had been killed, and Roman had been left alone to figure things out. It was a miracle he hadn't messed up dozens of times since he'd taken on the role, but that didn't mean his luck would hold forever.

Luckily, he wasn't completely alone anymore. He didn't have a mentor like Janice had been, but Arlene, the badger healer, had agreed to help him. They worked together almost every day, and that helped Roman feel better about his ability to help his people.

"Who's on our list today?" Arlene asked from the passenger seat of Roman's car.

Roman didn't like to drive, but since Arlene lived in badger territory, he had to pick her up every day. The badgers lived almost on the other side of the forest, so it was a bit of a trip, but Roman was happy to drive back and forth. If it meant someone was training him and that he'd be a better healer, he was ready to deal with much more.

"I got a phone call from Carla last night," he said, keeping his focus on the road. "Her youngest has a fever, so I promised I'd come around today. There's also Mrs. Wilson. She was feeling under the weather a few days ago. I told her to call me back if that didn't change, and while she hasn't, I'd feel better if I checked on her."

"Anyone else?"

"It's time to check up on Dean. I want to keep an eye on him since he's not a shifter. We don't know how his body will react to the pregnancy, so it's best to see him often."

"Good. I like to see you thinking ahead."

In this case, Roman didn't have a choice. Dean was his alpha's mate and almost as important as Jasper. He might be human and related to the foxes, but no one cared. Now that people were starting to realize that Jasper was nothing like his father, they wanted him to succeed. Everyone in the surfeit would benefit if he was a good alpha.

It had been a long time since the surfeit had thrived. They'd lived in fear for years, to the point that Roman could barely remember a time when he hadn't been afraid. He was twenty-four, and most of his years hadn't been easy. Jasper's father had never been a good alpha, which was why he was in jail. His beta, Harvey, was on the run, and the skunks were trying to rebuild. It wasn't easy because a lot of them couldn't remember what life had been like before Silas became alpha, but they were working on it. Jasper might not know what he was doing as an alpha, but whatever he came up with couldn't be worse than what his father had done.

Roman understood how Jasper must be feeling now that

he'd been forced to take his father's place. Being the alpha was a heavy weight, just like being the surfeit's healer, especially without training. Luckily, Jasper had Dean, and while Dean was human, he'd readily agreed to help Jasper guide the skunks. He had no idea what he was doing, either, but he was trying, and right now, that was what the skunks needed.

Dean was also very much pregnant, something he hadn't realized could happen. Dean had fox shifters in his family line, but he'd never been able to shift. Being human made his pregnancy more complicated, which was why Roman wanted to keep an eye on him. Luckily, Arlene agreed.

They first stopped at Carla's house. Thankfully, her daughter's fever had already broken. The little girl was still under the weather but was getting better, so Roman wasn't worried. He still made sure to glance at Arlene as he explained it to Carla, and since the badger healer didn't say anything, he knew she felt the same way.

She'd never allow him to hurt someone from his ignorance. He was doing his best but still had much to learn.

Mrs. Wilson was fine, too. Like Carla's daughter, she was more fragile because of her age. Shifters tended not to get sick easily, but it did happen when they were young or old. It was possible that Mrs. Wilson had the same illness that Carla's daughter had. Now that the old alpha was gone, the skunks were freer to mingle and become the surfeit they should have been since the beginning.

After Silas had become the alpha, things had changed. People were afraid of their alpha and of each other. They couldn't afford to be close to anyone in case they lost them or, worse, were betrayed by them. It would take time for the surfeit to heal, but with Jasper and Dean at their lead, they would.

The next person on the list was Dean, and Roman was a bit nervous. He'd never dealt with a carrier pregnancy before. Arlene had more experience, but never with a human. The badgers had been a safe haven for carriers when things in the forest had been complicated, and Arlene had taken care of all of them.

Roman made a mental list of things to check as he drove them toward Dean's house and parked in front of it. Arlene got out of the car and walked toward the house while Roman grabbed his bag. It took Dean a moment to open the door. When he did, Roman's gaze went straight to his stomach.

The pregnancy hadn't been obvious before, and it still wasn't, but Roman could see it. Dean had arrived in the forest with a human team sent to keep the forest under control and keep an eye on the alphas, so he'd been highly trained. With a stomach as flat as his, the first hints of pregnancy were already showing.

Dean caught Roman's gaze and rolled his eyes. "Jasper does the same thing."

Roman blinked. "What do you mean?"

"He keeps looking at me as if he expects my stomach to blow up or something."

Arlene snickered. "I think he keeps looking at you with hearts in his eyes. You're starting to show, Fox."

Dean pressed a hand over his stomach. "I am, aren't I?"

Roman and Arlene followed Dean inside. The house was very different from how it had been when Jasper's father was the alpha. Jasper and Dean were redecorating, and everything looked homier and more comfortable.

Dean flopped onto the couch. "What are you going to do to me today?"

"You speak as if you expect us to torture you," Arlene said.

"You might as well. This is still so fucking weird."

Roman could only imagine the shock it had been for Dean to find out he was pregnant. He'd lived outside of the forest before arriving with his team, and the carriers were a secret that the shifters had kept for a long time. Humans didn't know that some male shifters could get pregnant, and Roman hoped things would stay that way.

No one expected Dean to be able to get pregnant, but here he was.

"I just want to make sure everything is going well," Roman said.

"Do your worst," Dean murmured.

Roman didn't do his worst. Instead, he made sure he covered everything. He couldn't afford to have the alpha mate die on his watch, but more than that, he liked Dean. All of this might be new for him, but he was still doing a better job than the old alpha ever had. No one in the surfeit wanted to lose him, and it was Roman's job to ensure he and the baby were all right.

He'd make sure they were, no matter what.

Alvin's stomach growled, but he ignored it. It always growled these days, but then, it was usually empty. He was getting used to the sensation. Sometimes he was so hungry that he wasn't even hungry anymore.

He snorted quietly. That didn't make sense. Was he reaching the part of this where he had hallucinations? Could not eating for long enough create hallucinations? He didn't know, and he didn't want to find out.

He just wanted food.

He stared at the house beyond the trees. He'd been keeping an eye on the window at the back of the house because he knew that was where the kitchen was. He might hate that he needed to spy on people, but it was necessary, and if it meant he'd survive, he'd do it. He always tried to give people their privacy, which meant not spying through their bedroom windows.

The woman who lived here was cooking, and she was

probably too hot, because she'd opened the window. Her cheeks were red as she moved around the room, stopping a few times to talk to someone Alvin couldn't see. He'd been watching the house long enough to know she had children.

When one of the kids started crying, the woman quickly dried her hands and headed out of sight. This was Alvin's only chance, so he scrambled down the tree he'd been hiding in and toward the house.

His heart was in his throat as he leaned through the window. He quickly looked around, hoping to find what he was looking for. He sobbed when he saw the freshly baked loaf of bread on the counter. It was almost too far for him to reach, but if he pushed himself up and through the window just a bit more, he could get it.

He could hear the woman talking to her child, and he knew he didn't have a lot of time. He put his hands on the windowsill and tried to push himself up, but his arms couldn't take his weight. He was too weak because he hadn't been eating, but he pushed himself to the end of the little energy he still had. It took a few tries, but eventually, he got high enough.

Now came the hard bit. He tilted forward, the windowsill digging into his stomach. He ignored the sensation and snatched the bread from the counter, hissing when he realized it was hotter than he'd expected. He didn't let go, though.

He couldn't afford to.

He scrambled back out the window, almost falling on his ass. He didn't look back as he ran through the forest. He didn't stick around to see how the woman would react to finding out that the bread she'd baked for her family had vanished. Alvin hated that he was stealing from people, but this was the only way for him to survive.

He'd expected things to be hard when he'd decided to sneak into the forest, but he hadn't expected it to be like this. He probably should have, which meant he was a fool.

At the moment, he was a fool living in a forest full of shifters.

Luckily, the forest was vast, and even though many people lived there, there was enough space that he could hide without anyone stumbling onto him. He had to be careful because shifters would be able to smell him if they came too close, but so far, no one had found him, and he doubted anyone would anytime soon.

He'd been moving back and forth, so he didn't have a home base, but he did have a spot where he'd been sleeping the past few days. He'd have to abandon it soon, but he could sit there for a few more hours, eat bread, and rest.

That was what he did. As soon as he reached his tree, he climbed up into it. It was much harder than it had been when he first began using it. His arms were weak, and his legs felt like they couldn't support his weight. Eventually, he managed to settle onto the branch where he'd made his home. It was thick enough that he could sit comfortably and at a spot where the tree was slightly hollow, which meant he could fit his back into that hollowness. He'd slept here a few times without falling off, and it helped him feel safer than when he slept on the ground.

Alvin was salivating as he looked at the bread in his hands. The loaf was big enough to last him a few meals. It could be more, but he was too hungry, and he knew he wouldn't be able to resist. He should because it wasn't easy to find food, but his stomach growled again, and the bread smelled heavenly.

Alvin quickly tore the loaf into two pieces, hissing at the steam it released. It was so hot that it scalded his fingertips and his lips when he started eating, but he didn't care.

He was careful with the second half of the loaf. He wrapped it into one of his t-shirts that was still marginally clean and stuck it into his backpack. He forced himself to eat as slowly as possible, trying to make the sensation of having a full stomach last longer.

As he did so, he contemplated his options. He'd come here because he'd never found a place in the human world. It had taken him a few years to realize that was probably because he wasn't fully human. He'd grown up in the foster system, and it had been almost impossible for him to trace his family tree, but he'd started as soon as he'd been on his own at eighteen, and now, he knew.

His great-great-grandparents had been shifters. His great-grandfather had been one, too, but he'd married a human woman. Their children had been half-shifters, and Alvin's grandmother had married a human. Alvin's mother had been one-quarter shifter, which wasn't enough for her to shift. Alvin's father was human, so he knew he'd never be able to, either, but he didn't care.

He shouldn't feel as much of an outsider as he always had. He wasn't even half shifter. He was barely a shifter and would never be able to turn into an animal, but he'd never found a place in the human world. No matter how long and hard he tried to become part of it, he was always on the fringe of society.

After leaving the foster system, he'd struggled to find jobs and lived in dingy apartments with roommates. He knew his entire life would be like that if he didn't change something, so he'd decided to act.

Most people wouldn't have chosen to sneak into a forest full of shifters and live there without electricity or running water, but Alvin had never said he was smart. He definitely wasn't if the state his life was in was an indication of anything.

His stomach felt heavy as he finished his piece of bread, and he leaned the back of his head against the trunk of the tree. For now, he wasn't hungry anymore, but that would change. There was also the fact that it was still cold outside, and he was living in trees and sleeping on the ground. He was dirty and weak, and no matter how hard he thought, he couldn't see a way out.

He groaned and closed his eyes. He'd expected this to be hard, but it was even more difficult than he'd thought. He didn't know how to fix it. He'd created the problem by slinking in through a hole in the fence, and he realized how stupid he'd been, but he'd known this was his only chance to enter the forest.

Now that he was here, he felt like he would either die in the forest with no one to find him, or he'd be caught and kicked out, or maybe even worse, killed.

He didn't know what his options were. He wasn't even sure he *had* options. For now, the only thing he could do was survive, and he had every intention of doing just that.

He just wasn't sure he was strong enough to do it much longer.

CHAPTER TWO

"I think it's time we visit Janice's house," Arlene said. She'd been hinting at it over the past few weeks, especially since they'd visited Dean a few days ago, so Roman had known it was coming. He just hadn't expected it to come today. "We're in a hurry."

"We are, but from what you said, we might need some of the things Janice had at the house. You don't want to be unable to soothe a woman's pain while she's giving birth."

Roman grimaced. He definitely didn't want that, and while he'd helped Janice tend to women in labor several times, he'd be the one in charge this time.

It was terrifying.

He didn't think he'd be able to get through this if it hadn't been for Arlene. When Nora called earlier to tell Roman she thought she was in labor, he panicked momentarily. He'd almost expected her to give birth on the phone, but when he'd asked her how far along she thought she was, she'd laughed and told him it would be a while. This was her third child, so she knew what to expect.

That didn't mean Roman would abandon her to labor on her own. He'd called Arlene to warn her, and she agreed to be there during labor and birth. Roman would be in charge, but she'd help him if he needed it.

He was pretty sure he would.

"I don't think this is the right moment to go through Janice's things," he said. He kept his focus on the road even though his heart was racing.

"I agree, it's not, but we do need a few things I'm sure she had. Just park at her house. We'll get what we need and come back later."

Roman had been in Janice's house a few times since she'd vanished. That was how he'd known she was dead. He'd seen the blood, and even though he'd never found her body, there was no way she was alive. She wouldn't have stayed away from the surfeit for so long if she were.

He hadn't returned since then. It felt like he shouldn't and like he needed to keep the house the way it was so Janice could rest in peace. Her body hadn't been found, so keeping her house as untouched as possible felt like the only thing Roman could do.

It wouldn't last forever. He had his own place, but it was a bit out of the way, which wouldn't do if he was the skunk healer.

He softly snorted to himself. He already was the skunk healer. He might not have wrapped his mind around it yet, but everyone else had. He was the only person they called when they needed something. He was the only one they wanted to see when they felt sick. He was proud of that but also petrified because he had no idea what he was doing most of the time. He was only twenty-four. He wasn't supposed to be the skunk healer yet.

But there was no one else. He'd been apprenticing with Janice since he was fourteen. Back then, he'd only spent part of his time with her because he'd still been going to school, but as soon as he'd graduated, his apprenticeship had become full-time.

Six years didn't feel like enough to be in charge of the entire surfeit, but he didn't have a choice. He had to get as much experience as he could when it came to pregnancy and childbirth over the next few months because when Dean went into labor, Roman would be attending him.

Roman swallowed. He did as Arlene had ordered and parked his car in front of Janice's house. The place had looked gorgeous when Janice was alive, but now it looked as dead as she was.

All the windows were dark, and the yard Janice had tended to with love was dead. It was still winter, but things wouldn't get better with spring if no one was there to baby the plants.

Arlene didn't seem to have a problem with the house. She headed inside as if Janice was still alive, but Roman couldn't bring himself to do the same. Instead, he stayed outside, knowing this was supposed to be his house now.

The healer's house was always the same so that people knew where to find them. Once a healer retired, they could either stay with the new healer or move out. Roman had expected to make that move in a few years, when Janice decided it was time for her to slow things down. After she died, he'd refused to move in, even though he knew he should.

He still had no idea if he could do it. He wasn't sure he wanted to live where Janice had been killed. Jasper had had the house cleaned, so the blood was gone, but Janice had still died in the house. How was Roman supposed to live here?

The next few hours went by in a rush. Nora was further ahead than she'd thought, so Arlene and Roman got to work as soon as they reached her house. There was barely time to give her any painkillers. Her labor was fast and hard, and she had a baby in her arms after only three hours. She was exhausted but smiling, and even though Roman smiled back, he felt a bit dead inside.

Janice should be here. She should be the one doing this, not him.

"You did a good job," Arlene said as she and Roman watched the new baby and her mother.

Roman tried hard not to cry. "Janice would have done a better job."

"Maybe. She'd been a healer much longer than you have."

Roman rubbed his face. "I was never supposed to become the skunk healer at twenty-four," he complained.

Arlene squeezed his shoulder. "Maybe you weren't, but you're doing a great job. Janice would be proud of you."

Roman hoped she would be, but it didn't help him feel any less terrified.

What if he did something wrong? What if instead of helping someone, he hurt them?

His mind went to Dean. Dean was the alpha mate, and he was carrying the future alpha. Roman knew that wasn't how Dean and Jasper thought of their child, but it was the reality of it. One day, the baby in Dean's stomach would become the alpha after their father, and Roman would be responsible for their birth and keeping them healthy for the rest of his life.

The prospect was enough to make him want to run away screaming.

"You worry too much," Arlene said gently. "I know how you feel. I was in your place once. I think you would have felt like this even if Janice had retired instead of dying. Becoming responsible for everyone's health is scary, but you'll have to learn to deal with it. Eventually, you're going to spread your wings and do this on your own like you're supposed to. Until you feel ready for that to happen, I'll be there to help you."

Roman didn't know what he'd do without her. Probably hide in the forest and refuse to come out even when people needed him. In theory, he knew what he was doing, but actually doing it was far more complicated and scary.

He supposed he was getting there. It would take time and a lot of hard work, but he needed to have faith in himself. Janice wouldn't have chosen him as her apprentice if she hadn't thought he could be the best healer the surfeit needed and deserved.

It didn't matter that Roman felt he would never be good

enough. It didn't matter that he keenly felt Janice's loss and that he often didn't know how to deal with it. The only thing that mattered was that he was the skunk healer. There was no getting out of that, and deep inside, he didn't *want* to get out of it. This was what he'd always wanted to do since he was a child. He might not have thought he'd do it at twenty-four, but that didn't mean he couldn't do it.

He had to, for everyone's sake.

Alvin was on the move. He wasn't moving very fast, but at least he was moving, even though it felt like his legs might buckle under him at any moment.

Even though he was so hungry he was starting to wonder how tree bark would taste.

He shook his head and told himself to ignore his stomach. The loaf of bread he'd stolen a few days ago hadn't lasted long, but it had given him some energy. He'd decided it was time to move so he could be sure no one would find him, so he'd gathered the few things he owned and walked away from his tree.

He had no idea where he was. To be fair, he'd never had any idea where he was since he'd entered the forest. He'd re-searched the place before coming, so he'd known he was en-tering badger territory, but he'd been moving since then, and he didn't know how far he'd gone. He could still be in badger territory, or he might have reached the other end of the forest. There was no way for him to find out unless he wanted to talk to people, but he couldn't do that, even though he was lonely.

It was almost worse than being hungry. He'd never had many people in his life, or any, really. He had a few friends at school, but everyone had known him as the weird kid who lived in a foster home. He'd lost touch with everyone after he graduated, but he hadn't missed any of them. He doubted they'd thought of him twice since then, so the feeling was no doubt mutual.

This was another kind of loneliness. Even though he'd never been close to anyone, he'd still seen people daily. He'd gone to work, the grocery store, and places where people spent time.

But not since he'd snuck into the forest. Since then, he hadn't seen another human being, and he was starting to feel it.

That didn't stop him from freaking out when he heard the voices. He froze, frantically looking around. These people were shifters, which meant they'd be able to hear and smell him if he wasn't careful.

"When are we going?" a man asked.

The voice came from Alvin's left, so he moved to the right. He tried to be fast, but not so fast that he'd make noise.

"Everything needs to be in place before we go," a second man said. "We can't afford for the plan to fail. Silas needs us to get him out of jail, and we will. We'll only have one opportunity, so we can't waste it."

The voices came closer, so Alvin quickly hid behind a big tree. His heart raced, and he knew that if these guys heard him, they'd come after him — not because they were shifters, but because they sounded like criminals. They were talking about breaking someone out of jail, for fuck's sake.

That couldn't be good.

"I'm done waiting, Harvey," the first guy snapped. "You've been promising a lot of things since Silas was caught, but so far, none of them have been true. You were kicked out of the surfeit, and we've been hiding since then. I hate living in the forest."

"You should spend more time shifted." The second guy, Harvey, didn't sound happy.

"Are you calling me an animal?" the first guy asked with a

snarl.

Alvin shivered. Hopefully, they were distracted enough by each other that they wouldn't notice him.

Alvin wasn't surprised when his luck ran out. He hadn't realized the two guys weren't alone, and he didn't until he heard a new voice.

"Did you hear that?" the third guy asked.

"Hear what?"

"I think someone's spying on us."

Alvin bolted. He wasn't going to stick around and find out what was happening. He didn't care who these guys wanted to break out of jail. He just wanted out of here.

But these people were shifters. He had no idea what kind of shifter, but they were coming after him. The footsteps were loud behind him, almost as loud as the sound of Alvin's pounding heart in his ears.

He darted between the trees, stumbling over roots and catching himself over the hard tree trunks. He skinned one knee and tore one of his palms, but he didn't pause, not even when he started bleeding. He could still hear the three men behind him.

"Catch him!" one of them yelled.

There was a yip, and Alvin's stomach dropped.

He'd researched the shifters who lived here and knew there were coyotes, bobcats, and foxes amongst smaller and less dangerous shifters. They could catch up to him and hurt him badly, and it sounded like one of the shifters after him belonged to one of those species.

Alvin could have sworn he felt the breath of the shifters on his neck, and he realized he might well be right when something caught his leg. Fangs closed around the meat of his calf. The pain was sudden and searing, making him cry out. He stumbled forward and felt the fangs leave his body, ripping out some of the muscle. He turned, knowing he couldn't continue to run. They'd catch up to him eventually.

The only shifter he could see was one that looked like a dog, no doubt a coyote. The coyote had stumbled, and Alvin kicked him before he could get back to his feet.

That felt like it caused more pain to Alvin than to the coyote. Alvin had to grab the closest tree while he stood on his wounded leg because he would have fallen on his face if he hadn't. He couldn't afford to give in to the pain. He kicked the coyote again, aiming for the head. The coyote finally crumpled, and while he wasn't unconscious, hopefully, this would give Alvin enough time to run.

He turned and hobbled away. Every time he put down his wounded leg, he wanted to scream, but he was careful not to make too much noise. He was pretty sure the shifters would be able to find him by following the trail of blood, but he couldn't worry about that. He just had to continue moving, even though he was woozy and felt like the world was closing in on him.

His vision grew dark at the edges, and the trees in front of him danced. He raised a hand to catch himself, and it felt like it wasn't his. It was almost as if he was looking at someone else's hand, even though he knew it was his and that he was moving it.

He stumbled forward, but the pain was too much. The foot of his wounded leg caught a root, causing more pain to run up his leg. He fell to his knees, wondering how long it would take for the three shifters to find him. When they did, they would make sure he could never spy on them again, even though he hadn't done it on purpose.

He didn't care about whoever they wanted to break out of jail. He just wanted a place to call home and hoped he could find that here in the forest.

He should have known things wouldn't be that easy. They were never easy for him, and it made sense that even death wouldn't be. It would be painful and awful, and there was nothing Alvin could do.

He was alone in the forest, surrounded by people who would kick him out if they found him and being followed by shifters who were going to kill him.

Alvin always told himself never to give up, but this time, he did. He slid to the side, crying out when the movement jolted his wounded leg. He almost ended up face-first in the leaves on the ground, but he managed to land on his side instead. A leaf stuck to his cheek, but he didn't have the energy to brush it off. He didn't have the energy to do anything more than close his eyes and wait for death to come.

Chapter Three

R oman was exhausted. Nora and her baby were okay, but they weren't the last patients he'd seen today, and he couldn't wait to get to bed. He hoped no one would need him during the night, but if they did, he'd go, just like he should.

He really hoped he could get a full night of uninterrupted sleep.

He needed it. He'd been sleeping badly since Janice had disappeared, and even though things were getting better in the surfeit, his sleep was so light that just about any noise woke him up. He'd tried sleeping with plugs in his ears, but when he did, he was terrified that someone would knock on his door because they needed him, and he wouldn't hear them.

Not sleeping well meant he was more tired than he should be, which in turn might cause him to make mistakes. He'd never forgive himself if something happened to one of his patients because of that, which meant he had to get to bed.

He parked in front of his small house and turned off the engine. He felt like he didn't have the energy to get out of the car and into the house, and he stared at the night for a moment, wondering if he was too tired to care. Maybe he could sleep in his car.

He softly snorted and opened the door. He wouldn't be sleeping in his car. He didn't want people to be worried, which was what would happen if they found him there. The house was nearby, and he didn't even have to cook. He could grab a piece of bread, eat it at the counter, and fall into bed.

The sound of a branch cracking in the nearby forest made him jump. He stared in the direction from which the sound had come but couldn't see anything. It was probably an animal, although it sounded bigger than the animals that usually hung around here.

It couldn't be Harvey. Roman was afraid of what the old beta was up to, but he didn't have a reason to come after Roman. He was somewhere in the forest plotting something, but since Roman was only a healer, it was none of his business. If he ever found out what Harvey was up to, he'd go straight to Jasper, but right now, he only had a cracking branch, and he wanted nothing to do with whatever was out there.

He also wanted nothing to do with the moan that came after the crack, but it made him freeze in his tracks. He was a healer, and that had sounded like a moan of pain.

Roman squinted in the darkness and licked his lips. Was there someone out there? It sounded like they were hurt, and he couldn't abandon them if they were. He'd never forgive himself if he found a dead body tomorrow morning and knew he could have done something to help, but who could be out there moaning?

There was no way it was a surfeit member, right? Everyone was at home, having dinner with their family. They'd gotten used to not being out late while Silas had been the alpha, and they still hadn't shaken off that habit. Very few people hung around in the dark in the surfeit, but maybe someone had gone for a walk and got hurt.

Roman swallowed. He didn't want to go out in the darkness, but he wasn't sure he had a choice. He wasn't about to bother Jasper and Dean just because he'd heard a noise in the dark. He had no doubt Jasper would come, but he was getting some much-needed rest, and Roman didn't want to make him come if it was nothing.

Maybe it was an animal. That was what would make the

most sense, and while Roman wouldn't know what to do with a wounded animal, perhaps he could help it. If he couldn't, he'd call someone, but he couldn't until he knew what was happening.

There was another moan, much softer this time, as if the person or animal making it was losing energy. That got Roman into motion. He ignored his fear as he grabbed his bag from the car's passenger seat. He hauled it over his shoulder, took a deep breath, and moved toward the forest.

The night got darker when he stepped between the trees. He had no idea where he was going, but luckily, the light on his porch was on, which meant he'd be able to find his way home. First he had to find whatever was in pain, so he took out his phone and turned on the flashlight app.

Somehow, it made the forest even creepier. Roman might have lived here all his life, but he'd always been told not to leave the house after dark and to stay away from the forest. Not everyone who went into the forest at night came back, although no one knew what happened to them. Silas no doubt had something to do with it. It was too late to help those people, and Roman didn't want to know what the old alpha had been up to in the forest at night.

He moved forward, telling himself that whatever was making that noise needed him. He kept his attention on that, and he was so focused that when he finally found the man, he didn't recognize him as such for a second. His focus moved over a pair of legs sticking from under a tree and continued until he realized. He backtracked and stared at the shoes.

There definitely was someone here.

Even though Roman was terrified, he stepped closer. "Hello?" he called out. "Are you all right?"

Roman had unfortunately seen death before. As a healer, he'd had to deal with people dying. Most of them had been old, but Roman could see blood on one of the legs in front of him. This person was in pain, and it wasn't because they were old.

The person groaned softly but didn't move, and Roman rushed forward. No one was going to attack him. This person was the only one here, and they needed him.

He wasn't sure where to put his things so he could see better. He had to prop up his phone on a root. It didn't illuminate the person on the ground well enough, but Roman could see he was male, young, dirty, and way too skinny. His eyes were closed, and when Roman touched him, his skin was cold.

"What happened to you?" he asked, even though he didn't expect the guy to answer.

Maybe he wouldn't, but his eyes popped open. For a moment, they stared at each other. The man's eyes were brown and sunken in, and whatever had happened to him, it was clear he hadn't been fed. Roman didn't know the circumstances, but he didn't like it.

"I'm a healer," he said. "Don't worry. I'll take care of you."

The man continued staring. Roman didn't have anything else to say right now. He needed to focus on what his next move would be.

He had to examine the man's leg to know if it was safe to move him. It wouldn't feel great for him, but Roman didn't have a choice. He needed to know what he was dealing with.

Hopefully, whatever had wounded the man hadn't stuck around.

Was the man an angel? Alvin frowned at the thought. No, he was pretty sure the man had said he was a healer. He looked like an angel, though. Alvin could see his hair was blond, and he wanted to touch it, but he didn't. It would be rude without asking first, and Alvin wasn't sure he'd have the strength to do so, anyway. His body felt heavy in a way that didn't feel right, and when he tried moving, he couldn't.

Was he paralyzed? He might be. He didn't think so, though. He remembered what had happened to him, and he was pretty sure that between not eating for too long and losing a lot of blood, his body was just giving up. He was surprised he'd woken up when the healer found him. He'd expected to die and never wake up, yet here he was.

He kind of wished he *had* died.

His leg felt like it was on fire, and his entire body ached. The guy might be a healer, but that didn't mean he'd be able to help him, and even if he could, it would come with problems.

Alvin groaned and tried to sit up. The healer pushed him back down, but Alvin couldn't allow anyone to find him.

"I have to go," he said.

The healer shook his head. "You can't. I don't think you'd be able to walk if you tried, but you lost a lot of blood, so you need to stay where you are. I'm going to help you. I'll call someone to get you to my home and make sure you're okay."

Alvin shook his head. "You can't call anyone."

"I can't drag you to my home on my own, even though it's close by."

The man reached for his phone, but Alvin used the last of his energy to grab his wrist. The man looked shocked and stopped moving, and Alvin quickly let go.

"I can't be kicked out of the forest. No one can know I'm here," he explained.

"What? Why? What happened to you?"

Alvin couldn't tell him. If he did, he would get kicked out of the forest and back to the human world, and that was the last thing he wanted.

But he was pretty sure he would die if the guy didn't help him. Maybe it was stupid of him to cling to life as hard as he was. So what if he got kicked out of the forest? Was it better to die here than to have to find a way back? It would be harder the second time, but Alvin had snuck in once. He could do it again.

"Fine," the healer said. "I won't call anyone for now. I'll get you home on my own."

Alvin had been about to give in, but he'd take it. "My name is Alvin," he whispered.

He closed his eyes, wondering if he would ever wake up again. He felt closer to death than he ever had, but maybe his brain was being overly dramatic. Maybe this guy knew what he was doing and would save him.

Even if he didn't, it felt good to know that Alvin wouldn't die alone and that his body wouldn't be abandoned in the forest. Not that he would have cared since he'd have been dead, but at least now, he wasn't so lonely anymore.

"I'm Roman," the man said. His voice was soft and gentle, as if he cared about Alvin. "I'll take care of you, Alvin. I promise."

For some reason, Alvin believed him. He wanted to tell him that, but he couldn't open his eyes anymore, and when he tried to open his mouth, his lips didn't obey.

This was it. He was sliding into unconsciousness again and had no idea if he'd ever wake up.

Maybe he would, but he wouldn't be alone if he didn't. Right now, that was all he cared about.

Alvin had fainted, but at least now Roman had a name. He still had no idea what had happened to Alvin, but his panic had been clear when Roman had mentioned calling someone for help. It sounded like Alvin was running from someone and hiding in the forest, and there was only one person Roman could think of who would be in this position.

Everyone in the forest knew someone had snuck in

through a hole in the fence in badger territory. No one knew who that person was or why they wanted to be in the forest so badly, but Roman hadn't really been worried. He'd lived through harsh things in his short life, and a lone person walking around the forest hadn't scared him.

Even if that person was the one shooting at the alphas, Roman wasn't an alpha. Roman didn't think Alvin was the shooter, though. That had begun before the hole in the fence, but anyway Alvin didn't have a gun, and he was in such poor condition that there was no way he'd have the strength to shoot at someone. Roman didn't think he was dangerous, even if he was the guy who'd snuck in through the fence.

He still should call Jasper. Jasper was his alpha, and it was Roman's duty to report this kind of incident. He owed nothing to Alvin, and it would be easy to ignore his wishes now that he was unconscious.

Roman didn't want to. It didn't feel fair, so he decided to wait. He'd tell Jasper about this eventually, but Alvin wasn't dangerous right now, and Roman needed to focus on helping him. Maybe once he had Alvin in his home and had patched him up, he'd call his alpha and explain what had happened. In the meantime, getting Alvin out of the forest, cleaned up, and taken care of was essential.

Roman quickly examined the man stretched out on the leaves. He was cold and pale and needed food. He looked dangerously close to starving to death. Roman was worried about that, but it wasn't what worried him the most.

It was the wounds on Alvin's calf.

His jeans had been torn, but Roman had to open his bag and take out a pair of scissors to finish cutting them up. The fabric had stuck to the blood. Roman winced as he pulled it away, but Alvin didn't react. He was out like a light, which, on the one hand, was good because it meant he wasn't in pain, but on the other hand, not reacting to this kind of pain was worrying.

What the fuck had happened?

Roman moved his phone closer to the wounds on Alvin's leg. He tried cleaning them up, but he didn't have water in his bag, and it was really fucking dark. He could see it looked like something had bitten Alvin, though, which helped a bit. He was dealing with an animal bite, possibly a shifter's, but that didn't change much. He was planning to give Alvin antibiotics anyway.

There wasn't much he could do here, so after cleaning the wounds as best as he could and wrapping them up, he put everything away. He got to his feet, ignoring how his legs protested after having crouched for so long, and considered his next step.

He should call Jasper, if anything so he could have help getting Alvin back to his home, but he'd told Alvin he wouldn't call anyone. That meant he was alone and would have to drag Alvin back. There was no way Roman was strong enough to haul him into his arms, and that wouldn't change if he shifted. He wasn't a big shifter like a bear or a bobcat. He was a skunk, which wasn't of any help right now.

He swung his bag onto his shoulder, moved Alvin's body so it would be easier to drag him, and got to work.

Alvin never reacted. He never said anything as Roman panted and swore. He dragged Alvin toward the house by his armpits after tying a branch to his leg to keep it as immobile as possible, hoping he wasn't hurting him even more than he'd been hurt before. It was this or calling someone, though, and he wanted to know what had happened before he did so.

Alvin wouldn't be dangerous to him. He would barely be able to get out of bed, so Roman wasn't worried for his safety. It wasn't just the wound but also everything else. Alvin didn't have the strength to do anything to Roman.

It took what felt like forever to drag Alvin to the house and even longer to get him into Roman's bedroom. He didn't have a guest room, so he'd have to give up his bed, but that was fine with him. The couch was comfortable enough to sleep on for a while.

He didn't put Alvin onto the bed right away. Alvin was filthy, and Roman wouldn't be able to change the sheets once the man was in bed. He needed to clean him as much as he could before getting him in, so he left him on the carpet in the bedroom and headed to the bathroom. He removed his shoes and jacket and dumped everything on the floor before pushing up his sleeves and grabbing a bucket. He filled it with warm water and soap, grabbed a washcloth, and went back to his bedroom.

The clothes on Alvin were just as dirty as he was and stank, so Roman didn't feel guilty when he cut them up. It was easier to get them off Alvin's body like that, and when he did, he was horrified. Alvin was incredibly skinny. Roman could count his ribs without even trying, and the sight made him want to stuff a burger into Alvin's mouth. If he was the guy who'd snuck in through the hole, it was obvious he'd been hanging around the forest on his own since then, barely eating.

What would push someone to do something like that? Roman couldn't tell if Alvin was a shifter or human because he couldn't smell him, but he wasn't sure it made a difference. For some reason, Alvin had felt the need to sneak into the forest and starve himself almost to death instead of asking for help. He'd sounded sure he'd be kicked out if he tried, and maybe he would be, but would it be worth dying?

Roman would have a lot of questions for Alvin when he woke up.

He spent a while cleaning Alvin and had to change the water in the bucket three times before it was clear. Once he was sure that Alvin was as clean as he'd get him without putting him into the shower, he moved on to his next task, which was Alvin's leg. Roman had cleaned the area, so he knew what he was working with now.

The wound was deep, and the animal had bitten part of Alvin's muscle in the attack. It left the calf misshapen, and it would be weaker than the other even after it healed. Alvin would have scars, and there was nothing Roman could do about it. He'd do his best to help Alvin and keep him alive, but he couldn't work miracles. He doubted that even Arlene would be able to do anything about the scars, and he wasn't about to call her.

Roman could take care of Alvin on his own. He was the skunk healer. This was his job, and he knew how to do it.

He kept telling himself that as he went to work. Hopefully, by the time he was done, he'd actually believe it.

CHAPTER FOUR

For the first time since what felt like forever, Alvin was comfortable. He was hungry, but he wasn't cold anymore, and the ground under him wasn't hard. He hadn't felt like this in too long.

He jerked into a sitting position and quickly blinked the sleep away. He wasn't in the forest. That was why he was so comfortable. He was in a bed, surrounded by objects he'd never seen before. He didn't know this place, but it certainly wasn't his apartment back in the human world. He'd had to share his room with another guy, and neither of them had enough money to decorate.

This bedroom was cute and comfortable, the way Alvin would have wanted his bedroom to be if he'd been able to afford it. The bed was big, the sheets soft, and the yellow light coming from the nightstand illuminated the room in a soft way that made Alvin want to go back to sleep.

He couldn't. He had no idea where he was or what had happened. The only thing he could remember was a guy named Roman, who had found him and insisted he was a healer.

Had he called for help? Alvin hadn't seen much of Roman, but he hadn't seemed like the kind of guy who'd be able to drag him all the way here and put him into bed. Even if he was a shifter, he wouldn't be strong enough.

Alvin needed to get out of here.

He pushed the blankets away, shivered, and realized he was naked. Whoever had brought him here had stripped him and cleaned him up. He couldn't remember the last time he'd smelled so good, like flowers and cream.

"What are you doing?" Roman asked as he rushed into the bedroom.

Alvin hadn't been able to see Roman well in the forest, but he was sure this was him. He remembered thinking Roman was an angel, and even though Roman's blond hair was damp right now, he had that look.

Roman made a beeline for Alvin, his hands out as if he was going to stop Alvin from leaving. Alvin didn't listen to him and tried to push his legs off the bed, but a searing pain in his calf stopped him.

Right. He'd been bitten by a shifter, which was why he'd thought he was going to die.

"Where am I?" he asked. "Where are the shifters who were after me?"

Roman pushed Alvin back into the bed and helped him get comfortable. The pain in Alvin's calf pulsed in a way that made him want to throw up. He didn't think he was going anywhere, at least not right now.

"Is that what happened to you?" Roman asked as he quickly checked the bandages on Alvin's calf before tugging his legs back under the blankets and pulling them on top of him.

"Yeah. They came after me, and I'm pretty sure one of them was a coyote shifter."

Roman frowned. "A coyote? That shouldn't be possible."

"I know what I saw, even though I was terrified and running for my life."

"I'm not saying that's not what you saw, but you're in skunk territory. There's no way you went far with that wound on your leg, so you were attacked here, but coyotes aren't supposed to come into our territory without asking our alpha. I doubt Jasper allowed any of them in. Josiah might be doing a good job as their new alpha, but some of them are just bad people."

Alvin had no idea who Josiah was, and he didn't care. "I need to go."

Roman arched a brow and sat on the mattress next to Alvin's hip. He placed himself on top of the blanket, but while Alvin was trapped on that side, he could sneak out of bed on the other.

He wouldn't be going anywhere with Roman staring at him like this.

"Where do you want to go?" Roman asked.

Alvin swallowed. He could lie, but what good would it do? Roman had eyes. He could tell Alvin was in bad shape, and since he had to have been the one who'd stripped Alvin and cleaned him up, he'd seen just how bad Alvin's state was.

"I can't stay here."

"Because you think you'll be kicked out if anyone finds you."

Alvin nodded. "I'm not supposed to be here."

"I know. You're human, but if you were one of the few allowed to be in the forest, you wouldn't have been roaming the area on your own and starving yourself. You came in through the hole in the fence."

Alvin realized it was useless to deny it, but he couldn't say the words. What would happen if he did? Would Roman kick him out of the house? It was what Alvin wanted, but he doubted he'd survive it.

He'd been on his own for too long. He was weak and starving, and now he was also wounded. He'd probably get an infection and die if he left this place. He'd thought he would when he was under the tree, but now there was a chance he could survive, and he wanted that.

He wanted to live. He wanted to stay in the forest and build himself a life here.

But he didn't know if any of that would ever be possible. He was human, even though he had shifters in his family tree. Why would the shifters who lived here welcome him? Especially after he'd snuck in, he would understand if they kicked him out without listening to him.

Going back to the forest on his own felt like a stupid thing to do, but right now, it also felt like the only thing he could do. Maybe he'd die, but at least he'd do so in a place he felt he belonged.

That was all he'd ever wanted. He'd come so close to having it, but everything was over now. Alvin didn't know what would happen next.

But he wasn't done fighting for what he wanted.

Alvin was freaking out.

Roman wasn't surprised. Anyone would have been freaking out in Alvin's position.

Alvin was the person who'd snuck into the forest through the hole in the fence. Half of the forest was looking for him, while the other half was terrified that he was shooting people. It would make sense for him to believe he'd be hurt if anyone found out where he was.

Roman had many questions, but he could tell it would be better if he didn't ask them. He wasn't sure Alvin would answer, anyway. As curious as Roman was about him, he needed to make Alvin feel comfortable and at ease. Otherwise, he'd try doing something stupid like running and hurt himself even more.

The wound on Alvin's leg wasn't life-threatening as long as it didn't get infected, but it was pretty bad. Alvin needed to be careful and rest, not run around the forest. Roman wasn't sure he'd be able to convince the human of that, but he was going to try.

The first thing he wanted to do was get Alvin to be more comfortable with him. He wasn't sure how to do that. He'd never had to make friends before. For most of his life, he'd been isolated, like most people in the surfeit. They hadn't been allowed to leave their territory, and since the surfeit wasn't big, everyone knew everyone from birth.

Things had started changing after Jasper had taken power, and while Roman was getting to know people outside of the surfeit, it was slow going. So far, he'd only become close to Arlene and maybe Thomas, the badger alpha. There was Dean, of course, but he was different. He was part of the surfeit. Alvin was another matter entirely because, for one, he was human. Roman had never seen a human before meeting Dean, but Dean had shifter ancestry. If he didn't, he wouldn't be pregnant. Even though he couldn't shift, it was easier to feel closer to him.

As of now, there was nothing that made Roman feel closer to Alvin.

"Are you going to report me?" Alvin asked, his voice barely more than a whisper.

"Why should I report you?"

"Because you know I was the one who snuck in through the hole in the fence."

Alvin looked up.

Again, Roman was hit by just how thin the man was. It was the eyes. They were sunken in and surrounded by dark shadows. Roman wanted to feed Alvin and force him to get some sleep, but he couldn't.

No one should look like this, and no one should go through what Alvin had gone through. Roman didn't know why Alvin had thought it would be a good idea to sneak in through the hole, but to do something like that, he must have been desperate. Roman wanted to help him, which was impossible if he didn't know how to do so and what had happened.

"I haven't told anyone yet," he said.

Alvin gave a humorless chuckle. "Yet."

"I won't be able to get out of telling my alpha. He needs to know what's happening in our territory, especially after everything Harvey did. He's not a bad person, though. He's still trying to find his footing as the alpha, but he'll listen to what you have to say. I'm sure he'll see things the way I do."

Alvin frowned. "And how is that?"

Roman didn't know how to say it without being rude. "You're harmless. You can barely walk and are so weak that even I could knock you on your ass. I managed to drag you to my house and into my bed, and I wouldn't have been able to do so if you'd been in good health."

Alvin looked shocked. "Aren't you a healer?"

"I am."

"Are healers supposed to be so rude?"

Roman laughed. He liked that Alvin felt comfortable enough to tease him. It might not mean much, but maybe Alvin would stick around without Roman having to tie him to the bed. "I'm only rude when my patients deserve it."

"And I made you drag me all the way to your home."

"Pretty much. It would have been easier if you'd let me call Jasper."

"Jasper?"

Roman needed Alvin to see that this was the only way to make it work. He still didn't know what Alvin was trying to do, but he couldn't do it alone. He'd tried, and it hadn't ended well for him. Now, he was wounded and stuck in Roman's bed.

"He's my alpha," he explained. "He hasn't been the alpha for long, but he's a good person. I can't keep this secret from him. If I do, I'll end up in trouble, and I can't afford to let that happen. I'm the only healer the surfeit has. If I can't work, they don't have anyone to help them if they're ill or in an accident. I don't want to go against your wishes, but you won't leave me a choice if you don't agree to talk to Jasper."

Alvin stared at Roman for long enough that Roman didn't know how to take it. He had to be thinking about what Roman had said, but what decision was he making? Roman didn't want to hurt Alvin, but he couldn't hide this from Jasper and Dean.

Eventually, Alvin gave him a tight nod. "I'll talk to your alpha."

Roman was glad to hear that, but he could see Alvin was terrified. He probably expected Jasper to hurt him, which would have been true if the alpha had still been Silas.

But Silas was gone. He was in jail and couldn't hurt the surfeit or Alvin.

Roman got to his feet. "I'll go grab you some food," he told Alvin. "You clearly need it."

"You don't have to do that," Alvin quickly said.

"I know. I'm not doing it because I have to. I'm doing it because it's my job, and I want to help you."

Roman had lived all of his life with an alpha who would have let someone starve to death without blinking. He'd vowed never to be like Silas, and he was working hard to make sure he kept his compassion and empathy intact. He doubted he could ever be like Silas even if he tried, but it was so easy to start seeing other people as a bother or someone who didn't matter.

"Whatever you have is fine," Alvin said.

"Not really. I can see you haven't been eating in a while, so we'll start with something light. I have some chicken soup in the freezer."

Alvin's stomach growled, and his cheeks flushed. "Sorry about that."

"You have nothing to be sorry about. Get some rest while I heat the soup, all right? Once you have something in your stomach, it'll be easier for you to fall asleep and sleep through the night. I can't imagine you've done a lot of that in the forest."

"I can't remember the last time I had a full night of sleep," Alvin said, sounding like he was dreaming about it.

Maybe he was. Roman wanted to help him, even if he never found out why Alvin was in the forest. If that meant giving him a safe place to rest and heal, then Roman would do that.

As long as Jasper was okay with it.

CHAPTER FIVE

The days were getting longer, but it still got dark very early in the day. It wasn't that late, but the sky was pitch black, making it look like it was the middle of the night.

It wasn't, so Roman didn't have a reason not to call Jasper. He'd have one if he didn't get a move on and called, though. If he was going to tell him about Alvin, he needed to do so before Jasper and Dean headed to bed.

Roman had brought Alvin the chicken soup, some bread, and water. He'd told him to be careful and left him to it. He suspected that Alvin wanted to be alone for the meal. As long as he didn't eat too quickly, Roman didn't have a problem with that.

He could only imagine what Alvin had gone through. He'd been alone in the forest in the cold and darkness. He couldn't even shift, and it had to have been terrifying. Roman could only imagine what he would have done if he'd been in Alvin's place, and he wasn't sure he would have had better results than Alvin. Maybe it would have been easier for Roman to survive because he could have shifted. He'd still have had to hunt for food, though, and he'd always sucked at that.

Roman listened to the sounds coming from the bedroom for a bit but couldn't hear anything. He decided it was now or never, so he quickly took his phone out of his hoodie pocket and found Jasper's number.

"Please tell me there's no emergency," Jasper said when he answered.

"I'm really sorry to bother you," Roman told him.

"You wouldn't be bothering me if there wasn't something urgent you needed to tell me. Don't worry about it, Roman. Just tell me."

Roman sucked in a breath. "I found a wounded human in the forest and took him home. He's in my bed right now. He's the person who snuck in through the hole in badger territory."

The silence that greeted Roman's declaration was heavy. It made Roman wonder if he'd made a mistake, but he had to have faith in Jasper. He was nothing like his father, so he'd treat Alvin compassionately. If he didn't, he wasn't the alpha or the man Roman had thought he was.

"You found a human?" Jasper asked.

"Yes."

"You found a wounded human in the forest and decided to take him home."

He sounded like he couldn't quite believe it, and to be honest, neither could Roman. He shouldn't have done something that stupid. What if Alvin had been dangerous? What if he'd attacked Roman?

"He's in bad shape," Roman explained. "It's not just the wound on his leg, although that's a big part of it. He lost a lot of blood and part of his calf muscle. He's also frail. He hasn't been eating."

The sound of something heavy falling to the floor made Roman jerk. He turned toward his bedroom, and even without checking, he knew what had happened.

He swore and went to check on Alvin.

"What is it?" Jasper asked.

"I think he's trying to escape."

"Escape?"

"He didn't take it well when I explained he needs to heal before he can go anywhere. He's terrified someone is going to find him, which I guess makes sense since he's the guy who snuck in. He doesn't want you to know he's here, so I'm guessing he's trying to run."

Sure enough, when Roman walked into the bedroom, he found Alvin dragging himself toward the window. He was pushing himself forward with his good leg while the wounded one was stiff and seeping blood from the bandages. It would have made Roman laugh if the situation wasn't so dire. Alvin was so eager to run that he didn't care about the fact that he was ridiculous, crawling on the floor.

It was sad. Roman knew what fear was. He knew what it felt like to be terrified at every moment of every day. He never wanted to live through that again and wished no one had to.

That included Alvin. Roman didn't believe Alvin was dangerous. He might not understand why Alvin was here, but he was sure there was an explanation that Alvin would give eventually.

That was, if he didn't do something stupid and hurt himself while trying to run on one good leg and a bit of chicken soup.

Roman set his phone down and rushed to Alvin's side. Alvin jerked away when Roman touched him, but Roman ignored it and the sting of hurt it created in his chest.

"What are you doing?" he asked.

"I need to go. You called your alpha."

"I told you I would, but you have nothing to worry about. I promise Jasper isn't going to hurt you."

"Even if he doesn't, what about the others? He's going to have to tell someone, right? There's no way he can allow me to stay, even though he's the alpha. He has to answer to other people."

Roman helped Alvin into a sitting position. He was relieved that Alvin wasn't pushing him away, but he wished they didn't have to go through this.

"Put your arms around my neck," he ordered gently.

He expected Alvin to push him away, but he sighed and obeyed instead. With Alvin's arms around his neck, it was fairly easy for Roman to haul him to his feet. Alvin wobbled and would have fallen if Roman hadn't been there, but Roman *was* there, and he wanted to help.

They slowly made their way toward the bed. Roman made sure Alvin was comfortable amongst the blankets again before sitting on the edge of the bed. "You're right. Jasper does have to answer to other people. He's the one who guides the surfeit, but there are also people who guide the entire forest. They're called the council."

"And they'll kick me out."

"Maybe," Roman admitted. In fact, he was pretty sure the council wouldn't hesitate to kick Alvin out. They probably wouldn't even care that he was wounded and couldn't hurt a fly. "But Jasper isn't going to tell them tonight. He'll have to eventually, but it doesn't mean things are going to end as badly as you believe. You're here for a reason. Why don't you give us a chance?"

Alvin shook his head. "I can't give you a chance. Every time I give someone a chance, they hurt me, and I'm done with that."

Alvin obviously wasn't just referring to what had happened during his time in the forest. The pain he carried was deep, and Roman wished there was more he could do for it. As a healer, it was his instinct to help people, but there was nothing he could do for Alvin's soul. He could fix Alvin's body, but unfortunately, that was it. Alvin would have to do the rest.

But that wouldn't happen if he didn't trust people.

Alvin's goal hadn't been to make Roman angry. Roman was one of the rare people who had been kind to Alvin, and Alvin didn't want to lose that.

The problem was that Roman had called his alpha. That meant Alvin didn't have a lot of time left, and he needed to do something. It wouldn't end well for him if he was here when this Jasper guy arrived. No matter what Roman thought of his alpha, there was no way Alvin would be allowed to stay. At best, he'd be grabbed and locked up, then kicked out of the forest.

If he *was* kicked out, he'd find a way back in, but all of his hard work would have been for nothing. All of the pain he'd endured over the past few weeks would be wasted, and he didn't think he could stand that. Going back to the human world might mean he could organize better since he'd already lived in the forest for a while, but he didn't have anything out there.

Alvin didn't have anything in the forest, either, but he was sure he'd find something here. Even if it was just a place to call home, it would be enough for him.

"If I ask you, will you promise to not try to run again?" Roman asked.

Alvin didn't want to lie, so he stayed quiet. For some reason, Roman seemed to understand his answer, anyway. He smiled, and Alvin was glad he wasn't angry, but he didn't understand any of this.

Roman patted Alvin's knee. "No matter how often you try to run, you won't go anywhere until your leg is better. I don't think you'd go very far in the forest like this, although I suppose you're welcome to try."

Roman was right. How was Alvin supposed to do this? He couldn't run or even stand on his own two feet. He'd tried, and as soon as he'd put weight on his wounded calf, his leg had buckled. He'd known it was stupid, but he was stubborn, so he'd started dragging himself toward the window.

That was where Roman had found him. Luckily, he hadn't

been angry and wasn't making fun of Alvin. It was as if he understood why Alvin needed to leave and was even sorry that he couldn't help. Alvin was no doubt reading too much into it, but he liked Roman.

After finding him bleeding everywhere, most people would have left Alvin in the forest. Roman hadn't, maybe because he was a healer, or maybe because he was a good person. At some level, Alvin didn't want to disappoint him after he'd saved his life. Anyway, it looked like he wouldn't, because he wasn't going anywhere on his own.

Whatever came next, he'd have to deal with it. He couldn't run away, no matter how hard he tried.

"You have a few choices," Roman said. His tone was light, but there was a hint of steel in it.

"What choices?" Alvin asked cautiously.

"You can be good and stay in this bed until you heal enough that you can walk around on your own. This is my preferred option. I'll be by your side to help you the entire time, whatever you need."

"What's the second choice?"

Roman's smile was a little wicked. "I can tie you to the bed. That way, I'll be sure you're not going anywhere."

An image flashed in Alvin's mind, but it had nothing to do with his precarious position and everything to do with him being tied to the bed in very different circumstances. He shouldn't think of Roman this way, but now that he had, he wasn't sure he could ignore it.

Roman looked like an angel, but something told Alvin he was anything but. He wished the circumstances were different so they could explore this, but it was what it was. Eventually, Alvin would be dragged away from this place, and he'd never see Roman again. He couldn't put himself through that heartache, and he didn't want Roman to be hurt.

"I'll stay," he murmured, looking down.

"Good." Roman hesitated. "I'm not trying to hurt you. I want you to heal, which means allowing me to care for you."

Alvin didn't have a choice. He wouldn't be able to get anywhere even if he tried, so he might as well go along with whatever Roman was planning. Hopefully, that meant Roman would be on his side when people finally came to take Alvin away.

Alvin needed someone on his side, and he couldn't remember the last time he'd had that. It felt good, even though Roman didn't care about him. He just cared about his patient and keeping him safe.

A frantic knock on the door made Alvin jump. Roman's eyes widened, and he jumped off the bed, rushing toward the dresser. He'd had his phone in hand when he'd come into the bedroom to find Alvin on the floor, and when he looked down at the screen, Alvin realized he'd actually been on the phone with someone.

"I'll be right back," Roman said as he quickly left the room.

Alvin took a deep breath. He had no idea who was knocking on Roman's door, but he could imagine. It might be someone who needed a healer, but it might also be Roman's alpha.

If it was this Jasper guy, Alvin was about to find out what would happen to him.

For better or worse, he'd have to deal with it because he wasn't going anywhere. His leg wouldn't allow him to.

And neither would Roman.

Roman hadn't even reached the front door before it swung open and Jasper stepped in. The panic on the alpha's face made Roman cringe, and he rushed forward, raising his hands after pushing his phone into his hoodie pocket.

"I'm fine," he reassured Jasper.

Jasper fixed his gaze on Roman. He looked him up and

down as if trying to find a wound, but there was no wound.

"What happened?" Jasper asked. "One moment you were on the phone with me, and the next, I heard a commotion. You didn't answer when I called out."

"I'm really sorry," Roman told him. "I forgot I was talking on the phone with you when I found Alvin flat on his front on the floor. The idiot was trying to escape, even though he knew he couldn't."

Jasper's shoulders slumped just a bit, but he was still tense, as if he expected something to happen. He looked around, maybe trying to find Alvin, so Roman gestured toward the bedroom. "He's back in bed, and you don't have to worry about him hurting me. He couldn't even if he tried. He's too weak."

"Tell me what happened again," Jasper ordered.

Right now, he was an alpha, not just a guy trying to make the best with what he had. Becoming the alpha after his father couldn't be easy, but he was making it work. It was slow going, but no one had expected it to be easy. As long as he did things right and no one got hurt, Roman doubted anyone cared about how quickly Jasper settled into his new role.

"When I arrived home tonight, I heard a moan from the forest. I decided to go check it out."

Jasper pinched the bridge of his nose. "On your own?"

"I thought it was a wounded animal or something. I didn't think I needed to bother you or anyone else because an animal had decided to die behind my house."

"Maybe not, but call me the next time you hear something in the forest."

Roman nodded. He wasn't going through this a second time, so he was more than happy to agree with Jasper. "I swear I will."

"What happened next?"

"I went into the forest and found Alvin under a tree. He

was so still that I thought he was dead, but he opened his eyes when I crouched next to him. He had time to give me his name before he fainted, but he also told me not to call my alpha or anyone else."

"And you didn't think it was strange?"

"I knew it was, but I could tell he needed my help urgently. I knew he wasn't going to hurt me or run because of his leg, so I focused on taking care of him, and as soon as he was settled, I called you."

"So he's here right now?"

Roman nodded and gestured toward his bedroom. "In bed. I know you think he's dangerous, but I don't think he is."

"He's the person who snuck in through the hole."

"That doesn't mean he's dangerous, just that he was desperate."

"He's human?"

Roman nodded, but he'd thought about it. There had to be a reason for Alvin to want to be here so desperately. "He smells human, but it doesn't mean that's all he is."

Jasper nodded. "He might have shifter ancestry."

"It would explain why he wants to be here. If he doesn't have any family outside of the forest, he might have thought he could find one here."

"And there's no path for a human to ask to move into the forest at present."

Humans could only do so through the human government and military. Roman didn't understand how they worked, but he'd had the impression it wasn't easy. It would have been impossible for Alvin to get the authorization to move here, which would explain why he'd decided to do it on his own.

Jasper sighed. "This is a mess," he muttered.

"It is, but it doesn't mean it's a bad thing. Don't look at Alvin as the enemy. I don't think he is."

Jasper straightened his shoulders. "Well, either way, I'm about to find out. Take me to him."

Roman was surprised to realize he wanted to shield Alvin from Jasper. He didn't have a reason to. Jasper was a good person, and he wouldn't hurt Alvin.

But he might have to kick him out. Even though he had full authority over his territory, the council could try to work around him. It hadn't worked well when alphas had final authority before because they'd used it to hurt people, which was something the council was now trying to prevent. That meant allowing them more access to the territories, but it also meant giving them more power.

But Roman couldn't say no to his alpha. He guided Jasper toward his bedroom, hoping everything would be all right. He had to have faith in Jasper, and he did.

That didn't mean this wouldn't be a disaster.

Alvin was in bed like Roman had ordered. He looked cautious and paler than earlier, as if he expected the conversation to go badly.

"Jasper, this is Alvin. Alvin, this is Jasper, the skunk alpha."

Alvin blinked. "Is that what you are? A skunk shifter?"

"We both are," Jasper said as he stepped closer. "But you're human."

Alvin nodded. "I am."

"Why are you here, then? Why would a human want to live in a forest filled with shifters?"

Considering the shifters had been locked away in the national forests because humans didn't want anything to do with them, the situation made even less sense. Roman was curious to hear Alvin's answer, so he leaned against the wall and listened.

"I might be human, but it's not all I am," Alvin said. "There are shifters in my family tree. My great-great-grandparents were both shifters. My great-grandfather was a shifter, too, but he married a human. I can't shift, and I'll never be able to, but I don't fit in with humans. They rejected me ever since I was placed in the foster system, and they continued even after I aged out. The human world isn't the right place for me."

"And you thought the forest would be?"

Alvin raised his chin. "I know it is. I might not be able to shift, but it doesn't mean I'm fully human. I just need you to give me a chance."

"You didn't think it through when you decided to break in, did you?"

All of Alvin's defiance vanished as if it had never been there. His shoulders slumped, and his body language spoke of defeat. "I should have. I don't know what I expected to happen when I got in, but I guess I thought that eventually I'd find my way to one of your towns and find a place there. Instead, I've been roaming the forest since I entered it."

"And now you're in skunk territory, and you're injured. You were lucky my healer found you."

Alvin glanced at Roman. "I know. If he hadn't, I would have died under that tree."

Jasper sighed. "I'm going to have to report this to the council. If anything, they need to know we found the person who snuck in through the hole."

Alvin went white.

Roman knew this would happen, and he'd told Alvin, but it was still disappointing. Roman understood why Jasper needed to do this, but part of him wished the alpha didn't have to. It was easy to imagine what the council would do.

Alvin had never found a place in the human world, but maybe there was a place for him here, amongst shifters. Wouldn't it be fair to allow him to find it?

Humans and shifters would have continued living together if the forests were open. Alvin would have been able to find a place to call home from the beginning, and while it wasn't Roman's responsibility, he wanted to help him do so now.

But he might never get the opportunity.

Alvin had expected Roman's alpha to say that he needed to report his presence here. Jasper was in charge of these people, and they'd pay for it if he didn't follow the rules. They were Jasper's priority, not Alvin. Alvin didn't blame him for that.

But he still had something to say that might help Jasper pull to his side. "I heard something while I was hiding in the forest," he said.

Both Jasper and Roman stared.

"Does it have to do with whatever bit you? Was it a shifter or an animal?" Roman asked.

Alvin wasn't surprised Roman suspected it had been a shifter. "It does. I've been walking around the forest since I arrived, and I have no idea how much distance I covered. I tried to stay away from people, although sometimes, I had to steal food." Alvin looked down at his hands in his lap. "I'm really sorry about that, by the way."

"I think the food you stole is the least of our problems," Jasper said.

He sounded gentle, which Alvin hadn't expected. He wasn't sure *what* he'd expected from Jasper. Probably for him to kick him out as soon as he met him. He hadn't thought any of the shifters here would be nice to him, and he certainly hadn't thought he'd be allowed to move into the forest. He wouldn't have snuck in otherwise.

Alvin cleared his throat. "Right before I was wounded, I heard voices. Three guys were talking about getting someone out of jail." Alvin frowned, trying to remember more. "I think they mentioned someone named Silas. One of the guys,

Harvey, was trying to convince the others to have more patience." Alvin looked up, hoping this would be enough. "They heard me," he continued. "They came after me, and one of them was some kind of dog shifter. He's the one who bit me."

Roman's eyes went wide, while Jasper's expression had set. His jaw was tense, and Alvin could see he was gritting his teeth. He didn't know what he'd just said that had caused both of them to react this way, but he hoped they wouldn't take it out on him.

"A coyote," Roman said. "That's what bit you. Not a dog."

Jasper rubbed his face. "At least now we know Harvey is up to something," he muttered.

"We already knew he was up to something," Roman told him. "But I didn't expect him to still be in the area. I thought he ran to one of his friends."

"It sounds like his friends came to him."

Roman nodded. "They're planning on freeing your father."

Alvin's stomach dropped. How was Jasper's father involved in this? He didn't understand and was afraid to find out, so he didn't ask. He'd told Jasper everything he knew. He hoped it would be enough and that Jasper would allow him to stay, but he'd find a way back in if he didn't.

This could be Alvin's home. Alvin knew it, and he'd do everything in his power to be allowed to settle here. Sneaking in through the hole in the fence probably hadn't been the best idea, but no one had ever said he was smart.

He wasn't. He was desperate, which meant that he was ready to do pretty much anything to get what he wanted.

Jasper sighed and stared at Alvin. Alvin could see how conflicted he was. He might not know a lot about shifters beyond what humans were told in schools and what they saw on TV, but he'd tried to learn as much as he could before coming here. He knew what an alpha was, so he was aware of how complicated the situation was. Jasper seemed like a good person, and he was probably torn between protecting his people and wanting to do what he felt was right. Alvin wouldn't blame him if he decided to hand him over to whoever was in charge. He wouldn't even be surprised.

"I'm going to allow you to stay with Roman for a bit," Jasper said. "Roman says you're not to be moved, and since he's my healer, I believe him. He'll keep an eye on you while we try to decide what's next. You're not allowed to leave the house, though."

"I couldn't even if I tried," Alvin said quickly.

Roman snorted. "And he did try. He fell on his face. You don't have to worry about him running away, because he won't be able to."

Jasper nodded. "I'm still going to have to warn the council, but hopefully they'll realize Alvin isn't dangerous, especially while he's still healing. I'll make sure they know that attempting to move him would hurt him. We have more important things to focus on, and so do they, so hopefully, they won't focus too much of their time on him."

"Do you think your father is aware of what Harvey is planning?"

Roman and Jasper both sounded worried, which, in turn, made Alvin worry. What was happening? What had he gotten himself into? He was in the middle of a situation he shouldn't be involved in, and he had no idea what to do about it or even if there *was* anything he could do. Part of him wanted to leave and ignore all of it, but as Roman had pointed out, he wasn't going anywhere.

"Probably," Jasper said. "Knowing him, he's the one who came up with their plan. At least now we know what Harvey's up to. We don't have enough details, but I'm sure we'll find out soon enough. Harvey isn't going to wait forever. My father isn't a patient man."

Jasper turned his attention to Alvin. "Roman will keep an eye on you. If it wasn't for him, I'd already be calling the council, so you should listen to what he has to say. He'll take care of you and ensure you're healing and will recover, which you obviously need."

"Is that your way of telling me I look awful?" Alvin asked. He wasn't sure where he found the courage to tease the alpha, but here he was.

Jasper grinned. "If the shoe fits."

Alvin was overwhelmed. He hadn't expected Jasper to allow him to stay and didn't know how to thank him. Even if eventually he was dragged away from this place, at least he'd have some time to rest. He'd be fed and have a roof over his head, which he hadn't had in a while. Living in the forest for weeks had made him realize this life wasn't for him, but he didn't know if he could find a way out of it.

"I won't hurt Roman," he said quietly. "He helped me, and I never wanted to hurt anyone."

"See that you don't," Jasper said.

He didn't ask Alvin to promise not to try running away. Alvin wasn't sure if that was on purpose. He had every intention of attempting to run if he could, but he wasn't about to say it out loud. He was pretty sure both Roman and Jasper knew, anyway. They weren't saying anything about it, but that didn't mean they couldn't read Alvin like an open book.

"I'll see you soon," Jasper said as he approached the door. "Roman, you know where to find me. Call me or Dean if you need anything, although I'd rather you call me."

"I will."

Alvin dropped back against the pillows. This had gone much better than he'd expected, but he had no idea what would come next. Not knowing was terrifying, but at least for a bit, he'd be safe and warm.

He couldn't stay here forever, but for now, he'd found a

home.

CHAPTER SIX

R oman left Alvin in the bedroom and walked Jasper to the front door. The two of them were silent, and Roman didn't have to ask to know what Jasper was thinking about.

Silas was ruining their lives even from the cell he was in. He'd always been a nasty man, but Roman had thought the surfeit was finally free of him after he'd been locked up.

He should have known better.

Silas was pulling the strings from his cell, and Harvey was doing his bidding. It was good that Jasper had finally realized that the old beta was manipulating him, but with Harvey on the run, they couldn't keep an eye on him. That made him dangerous, especially now that they knew what he was planning.

Jasper had to tell the council. He'd have to explain how he knew about Harvey's plan, which meant he'd have to tell them about Alvin. Roman had expected that, but he couldn't help but wonder what the council would do.

Alvin was harmless. Even if he wasn't weak and wounded, he hadn't struck Roman as the kind of person who would hurt anyone. He just wanted to be allowed to live in the forest, and he'd done it the only way he could think of. It hadn't been smart to sneak into the forest, but sometimes, desperation made people do things that weren't smart.

Like going into the forest all alone because of a possible dying animal.

Roman was glad he'd followed his instincts. If he hadn't, Alvin would have died, and Roman wouldn't have been able to forgive himself. They would have found his body eventually, so he'd have known.

But Alvin would be okay. He'd need time to heal, both from the wound on his leg and from what he'd done to himself by not eating, but eventually, he'd be back to the man he'd been before. Roman didn't know what would happen then, but he hoped the council would see that Alvin didn't want to hurt anyone.

"This is a mess," Jasper murmured as they stood by the front door.

"I'm really sorry to make your life even more complicated," Roman said.

Jasper shook his head. "You did the right thing by bringing him here. He would have died if you hadn't."

"Your father would have killed him on sight."

"Good thing I'm not my father."

Roman wanted to ask if Jasper thought Harvey would succeed in freeing Silas, but he didn't want to find out. He already knew the answer. He was sure that if Harvey and Silas worked together, Silas would end up free, and everyone in the forest would be in trouble, especially the surfeit.

And Jasper.

They all had so much to lose now. Even though Silas hadn't been in jail for long, the surfeit had started healing. Jasper had fallen in love with Dean, and they were building a family. Everyone would have so much to lose if Silas ever came back, and Roman was sure that was what the old alpha wanted.

Roman had grown up with Silas in his life. He knew the man from having watched him for two decades, so he suspected he knew how Silas felt. The surfeit had been taken from him. The skunks were his property, and he wanted them back. He'd do everything he could to get his hands on the surfeit again, and that meant defying Jasper and the council.

"Dean wanted to come, but we had no idea what was

happening, so I told him to stay home," Jasper said. "He'll be frantic by now."

"You should go home and reassure him."

Jasper nodded, but he still hesitated. "I could have Alvin moved," he offered. "I know you said he's harmless, but I don't want you to feel like you need to be careful in your home. We could move him somewhere and have a few guards keep an eye on him."

Roman shook his head. He didn't even need to think about it. "I'm fine with him staying here. He wouldn't hurt me even if he wasn't wounded."

"I'm not sure why you feel that way, but I trust you."

Logically, Roman knew that, but it still hit him like a truck. He looked down at his feet, trying not to show Jasper that he was about to cry. It felt good to know that instead of wanting to control him, his alpha trusted him.

"I already called Arlene," he said, hoping to distract himself. "She'll come around tomorrow. I assured her that Alvin would be fine until then."

Jasper looked toward the bedroom. "What happened to him?"

"Well, I don't know for sure, but I think he's telling the truth. He lived in the forest for a while and basically starved, and then Harvey and his people found him. The wound is going to take some time to heal since his body is so weak, and while he tried running when I was on the phone with you, he couldn't even get to the window. You don't have to worry about him leaving or hurting me. He doesn't have the strength to do any of that."

"I suppose I should be happy about that. This entire situation is a mess."

"It is, but I have faith in you. You'll untangle it. And in the end, everyone will be safe and happy." The trust between them went both ways, and Roman wanted Jasper to know that.

He could only imagine how hard and complicated it was to be in Jasper's place. He'd always known he'd eventually be the alpha, but there was no way he'd expected it to happen so soon or in the way it had unfolded. People didn't trust Jasper's father, and they didn't know Jasper. It would take time for people to open up to him and allow him to be a true leader to their surfeit.

"Thank you for that," Jasper said with a smile. It quickly turned into a grimace. "Unfortunately, I have to contact the council about Alvin. He snuck in through the fence, and a lot of people have been looking for him."

"As long as you tell them he can't be moved. I understand why you have to, and so does he."

"I might not know him, but it doesn't mean I want to kick him out. He looks lost, and I understand how that feels."

They all did. For a long time, Roman had been lost, too. He was finally starting to find himself, but it would take time, and he could do so only if he was afforded the peace and tranquility he needed. That wouldn't happen if Silas came back.

Hopefully, the council would find Harvey before he could do something as stupid as letting Silas out of the cell he was locked in. Unfortunately, something told Roman they hadn't seen the last of Harvey and Silas.

The thought was terrifying.

Alvin wished he could listen to the conversation between Roman and his alpha, but there would be no getting out of bed for him. If he tried, he'd probably end up flat on his face, and that had already happened once earlier. He wasn't looking forward to it happening a second time.

He was fucked, and not in a good way. There would be no escaping this. He wasn't getting out of bed until Roman said he could, and he suspected it would take a while. His body didn't *want* to get out of bed, anyway.

He needed rest and food, and staying here would give him both. Unfortunately, it would also get him kicked out of the forest, but that wasn't something he wanted to think about. For now, he was exactly where he'd wanted to be when he'd decided to sneak into the forest. He'd deal with everything else later, once he had the strength to do so.

"How are you feeling about the situation?" Roman asked as he walked back in.

"I'm torn between being desperate and hopeful." Alvin didn't see a reason to lie to Roman. Roman already knew how Alvin felt, anyway. It had to be obvious after Alvin begged Jasper to allow him to stay.

Roman nodded. "I get it, and I want you to know that you can trust Jasper. I realize it's not as easy as saying it, but he's a good person."

Alvin believed that. Jasper had come running when he'd thought Roman was in danger, and he hadn't even known what he was getting himself into. He'd thought Roman needed help and had been there to provide it. He'd also allowed Alvin to stick around for a bit, at least until he healed, which was more than Alvin had expected. Most other people would have kicked him right out, but not Jasper.

None of that meant that Alvin trusted Jasper. He didn't know who to trust right now, and he had doubts even about Roman. The problem was that he didn't have a choice.

Roman patted Alvin's ankle. "I'm going to get you more food. You should try to sleep after that, and I'll do the same, because I have patients to see tomorrow."

Which meant Alvin would be alone in the house, unless Roman worked from there. That didn't sound practical since he was a healer, and Alvin hoped he'd have the opportunity to try sneaking out again. He wasn't strong enough right now, but maybe he would be in a few hours or tomorrow.

He'd promised not to hurt Roman, but he hadn't promised not to leave, or at least not to try to leave. He was pretty sure Jasper had noticed it, yet he hadn't said anything. Roman probably was right that Alvin wasn't going anywhere, but that wouldn't stop Alvin from trying.

He followed Roman's orders for the rest of the evening, eating when Roman told him to and allowing the healer to help him to the bathroom. One trip to use the toilet was enough to make him feel exhausted, and he was pretty sure that meant he wasn't going anywhere, but it wasn't enough to convince him not to try.

He dozed off after dinner, telling himself he was just resting his eyes so he'd be ready to leave as soon as Roman was asleep, but he fell asleep, and when he opened his eyes, the house was dark and silent.

Alvin's heart raced as he glanced around the bedroom. Roman was nowhere to be seen, which would allow Alvin to sneak out. He'd probably have to use the window, but that should be fine.

That was what he told himself as he slid to the edge of the mattress and threw his legs off the side. Pain pulsed in his leg, and his heart shot into his throat. He told himself he wasn't going to throw up, but it was a near thing.

He stared at his legs for a moment, trying to find a way to do this without hurting himself. He decided to stand on his good leg and did so without too many problems. The next step was more problematic. He'd have to put his weight on his wounded leg, which was going to be painful.

Alvin clung to the side of the bed as he did so. It only lasted a few seconds because his wounded leg buckled under him. It couldn't hold his weight, which meant he couldn't walk away from this like he'd been planning to.

He panted as he clung to the bed and tried to get himself

back onto the mattress. Luckily, he hadn't fallen on his face, but it had been a close thing. It took all of the strength in his upper body to haul himself back onto the mattress, and when his ass finally landed on the sheets, he sucked in a breath and tried to calm his racing heart.

Okay, so leaving the house was out. That meant he was stuck here, which wasn't something he was happy with. With the way his leg hurt, he suspected he'd need a lot of time to heal, and by the time he was strong enough to sneak out, the people in charge here in the forest would probably already have decided to kick him out.

He flopped back onto the pillow. He'd known this was a possibility when he'd snuck in, but he'd truly thought he'd be able to avoid getting caught. With his leg in the state it was in, there would be no running or hiding. The only thing he could do was stay in this bed and wait for the inevitable to happen.

His eyes prickled with tears. He hated this. He just wanted to show these people that he wasn't dangerous and could contribute to life in the forest. He wasn't sure how, but he knew he could.

He wasn't the enemy. He wanted a place to call home, and even though living in the forest had been hell, he'd truly thought he'd found it. Now, he suspected he hadn't. He was so tempted to give up. Part of him just wanted to lie back in bed and let Jasper and whoever he answered do whatever they wanted with him.

But another part of him wasn't done fighting. He just needed to get better. He had to believe that everything would be all right in the end.

He had to.

CHAPTER SEVEN

R oman was relieved when he opened the door to Arlene. He was pretty sure that his assessment of Alvin was correct, but that wasn't going to cut it in this situation. He had to be a hundred percent sure of what was happening, and that meant calling Arlene.

She looked at him with fond exasperation. "What did you get yourself into this time?"

It reminded Roman of Jasper and the conversation they'd had last night. "I thought it was a dying animal," he explained as he led Arlene into the house. "I wasn't going to call you for a dying deer or something."

"You got more than you bargained for."

Roman rubbed the back of his neck. "Yeah. Alvin definitely isn't a deer."

"Tell me about him."

Roman watched as Arlene took over his table in the kitchen. She placed her bag onto it and started taking things out, and he stayed out of her way. He told her everything he knew about Alvin, including things Alvin had told him after he'd woken up. He explained about the time Alvin had spent alone in the forest, starving and stealing food. Arlene made small sounds and noises, but Roman had no idea what she was thinking.

"So a coyote bit him?" she asked when Roman reached that part of the story.

"A coyote shifter, or at least, we're pretty sure it was a shifter. Alvin heard three men talking, so I doubt a wild

60

coyote ran after him. It would be too much of a coincidence."

"Which means Harvey has allied himself with other kinds of shifters. I'm not surprised."

Roman wasn't, either. There were plenty of bad people in the forest. Most of the alphas who had fought the council and their allies had died, but Silas hadn't.

Sometimes, Roman wished he had. It might make him bad, but he didn't care. Silas had never been a good person, and he'd ruined countless lives. Roman wouldn't shed a tear for him when he died.

Arlene looked down at the table and nodded, clearly satisfied. "Introduce me to your new friend," she ordered.

Roman led the way to his bedroom. Arlene grabbed a few things from the table, but nothing that would suggest that she didn't trust Roman's decisions about what he thought of the wound and how to treat Alvin. She was checking on him because Roman had asked, nothing more.

"This is Arlene," Roman explained as they entered the bedroom. "She's an experienced healer, so she'll make sure I did everything correctly. Arlene, this is Alvin."

"You were lucky Roman found you," Arlene scolded Alvin. "You would have died if he hadn't."

Alvin stared at her with wide eyes. "I'm aware."

Arlene narrowed her eyes. "Then, if you know what's good for you, you'll obey his orders and stay in bed as long as he feels it's necessary. Now show me your leg."

Alvin obeyed. Roman had to bite his lower lip so he wouldn't smile. Alvin had protested yesterday when Roman had examined him, but he didn't make a peep when Arlene did so. It was clear who was in charge, and it wasn't Alvin.

Arlene was almost done when someone knocked on Roman's door. He frowned, not expecting anyone else, and left Arlene and Alvin in the bedroom to open.

He wished he hadn't as soon as he saw who was on the

other side of his front door. "Council member," he said, already knowing why she was here.

Olga looked uncomfortable, although Roman suspected it wasn't because of him but rather because of the two other council members with her. "Roman," Olga said. "Jasper called me this morning. He explained what happened last night."

"He told you about Alvin."

"He did, and we decided we needed to see this man," one of the other council members said.

It was clear he wanted to push past Roman, but Roman stood his ground.

"My name is Roman, and I'm the skunk healer."

The way the man stared at Roman told Roman he wasn't happy.

"This is Ronald, the bat council member," Olga said. "And this is Karen, the new porcupine council member."

"We want to see the human," Ronald said.

Roman wished he could say no, but these were council members. They had authority over the forest and him.

It didn't used to be like that. When Silas was the alpha, these two council members wouldn't have been allowed in his territory. Things had changed, and that was good, but Roman was wary.

He let them in. He didn't have a choice. He guided them toward the bedroom, ignoring the glances Olga kept shooting at him. It seemed she wanted to talk to him, but he wasn't sure what she wanted to say. He suspected she was in the same position as he was. Neither of them had a choice about what was happening.

Ronald didn't seem to have a problem barging into someone else's house. He walked into the bedroom without even knocking, but Alvin was covered. The only thing out was his leg, and Arlene was still leaning over it.

When she heard Ronald, she looked up and glared at him in a way that made Roman feel like a naughty child caught doing something he shouldn't have. It gave Ronald pause, too, which was good to see.

"Healer," he said.

"Ronald. What are you doing here?"

"I don't know what you were told about the man you're working on, but he's a human who snuck in through the hole in the fence."

Ronald said it as if he expected Arlene to scream and jump away from Alvin, but she didn't. Instead, she looked at Ronald like he was an idiot.

"I'm well aware of who he is. It doesn't explain what you're doing here."

"We came to talk to him," Karen said. "We have to find out more about his reasons to be here and what he's planning."

"He needs to leave," Ronald interjected. "He's a danger to everyone in the forest."

Arlene snorted. "Is he? Because he's not getting out of bed anytime soon."

"You won't be the one to decide that."

"I will." Arlene straightened her back. "As of right now, Alvin is one of my patients. That means I'm making decisions for him, and he's not going anywhere. He can't walk, and he can barely stand up. He's weak because he hasn't been eating, and a coyote shifter bit off half his calf last night. He's in pain, and the wound on his leg will take a while to heal. Are you really going to kick a wounded man out of the forest?"

Ronald looked like he wanted to say yes, but he had to realize it would be a bad idea. Arlene might only be a healer, but everyone in the forest respected her. It wasn't the first time she'd worked for the skunks, and Roman was pretty sure she'd worked for the bats before, too. If Ronald opposed her, he and the bats would be in trouble.

Ronald turned to Alvin. "He might not be able to move, but he can answer our questions."

Roman knew immediately he couldn't prevent this. Alvin had to talk to the council members, whether he wanted to or not.

But he didn't have to do so alone.

Roman moved to the head of the bed. He wanted Alvin to know he was there for him. He couldn't do much against a council member, but he could help with moral support.

He didn't understand why he wanted to protect Alvin so badly. Maybe it was because Alvin was wounded, and the part of Roman who was focused on that knew he was fragile. Roman liked Alvin, and while he couldn't understand what not having a place to call home felt like, he knew how hard it was not to feel safe. He'd never felt safe in his life until Jasper became the alpha, and he didn't want Alvin to feel like he needed to run and hide again. It might make him an idiot, but he didn't care.

He didn't think Alvin was manipulating him. He also didn't believe that Alvin would hurt him or anyone in the forest. He just wanted a place where he belonged, and if the council gave him a chance, he might find it here.

Alvin was curious about these people but still wished he didn't have to talk to them. He'd been told what the council was, so he knew they had the power to kick him out of the forest. From the look of it, at least one of them couldn't wait to make that happen.

Since Arlene had mentioned the man's name, Alvin knew that Ronald was the one person he'd have to convince to leave him be. That was easier said than done. It was clear from the man's expression that he couldn't wait to find an excuse to drag Alvin out of there. The only reason he hadn't yet was

Arlene. She kept glancing at him defiantly, as if silently daring him to try it.

Alvin hoped Ronald wouldn't.

Unfortunately, Ronald turned his attention to Alvin. It made Alvin want to run, even though he couldn't. Arlene didn't seem to care. She kept poking at the wound in Alvin's leg, and Alvin was doing his best not to look down. He didn't want to see what his leg looked like, but he did notice the way the two women peered at Arlene's work. One of them paled so quickly that Alvin wondered if she was about to faint.

"What's your name, human?" Ronald asked rather rudely.

Alvin told himself he couldn't tell the man to fuck off. That would ruin all his chances to be allowed to stay.

"Alvin."

"What are you doing here, Alvin? Are you here to invade the forest? Are you the person who's been shooting at our alphas?"

Alvin blinked. "Someone's shooting at your alphas?"

Ronald snorted. "Don't play innocent. It can only be you."

"Why?"

"Because you're the only person who snuck into the forest. What was your reason for it?"

"Not killing your alphas. I don't care about them." Well, he didn't care about most of them.

Alvin did care about Jasper, even though he barely knew him. Jasper had given him a chance, and he hadn't kicked him out. He was on Alvin's good side. Ronald, on the other hand, was quickly getting on his bad side.

Did the man really have to be so rude and condescending? He stared at Alvin as if he were an insect on the ground that he couldn't wait to kill. Alvin suspected that Ronald hadn't kicked him out yet because he wasn't allowed to. He might be a council member, but he had to answer to the other council members. He couldn't make decisions on his own. If he could have, Alvin would already be out.

Alvin was sure of that.

"Alphas are important. Everyone cares about them," Ronald insisted.

"Not me. I'm human, and alphas don't mean much in the human world. I mean, I like Jasper, but he's the only alpha I've ever met."

Ronald looked like his head was about to explode. Alvin didn't mean to be rude, but he had to be honest. He could tell that Ronald would find him lacking if he wasn't. If Alvin wanted to convince these people he should stay, he'd have to work hard. Hopefully, being honest would be enough for them to at least give him a chance, but he doubted that would be the case with Ronald.

"Why did you sneak in, then?" one of the women asked.

Arlene made a sound of impatience. "Why do you think he did, Karen? He wants a better life, just like everyone else."

"And he thought he'd find it in the forest?" Ronald asked.

Alvin cleared his throat. He didn't want everyone's attention on him, but if they were going to talk about him, he might as well answer these questions. "I have shifters in my family tree," he explained. "Not close enough that I'm able to shift, but I've always felt I didn't belong with humans. I decided to see if I could belong here."

Ronald stared. Alvin wondered what was going through his mind, but he was pretty sure he didn't want to find out. Thankfully, Ronald wasn't the next one who spoke.

The third woman leaned forward, looking interested. "What kind of shifter?"

It was the first time anyone had asked Alvin this. "Opossum."

The woman leaned back, nodding. "We do have opossums in this forest."

"That doesn't mean he should be allowed to roam the

forest on his own," Ronald snapped. "Even though he has opossum genes, he can't shift and never will. He's not a shifter. He's human, and humans don't live here."

Arlene cleared her throat. "I beg to differ. I know plenty of humans who live here, and not all of them have shifters in their family trees. If you want to be strict, Alvin is one of the few who *should* be allowed here."

Ronald's face went red again. It was entertaining to watch, but Alvin told himself not to look smug. He couldn't deny he liked that Arlene was smacking down Ronald, though. The man might have a job to do, but he was incredibly rude and had clearly already decided what to do with Alvin.

"Anyway, this conversation is useless," Arlene continued. She was finally done poking at Alvin, and she'd started to bandage his leg back up. "He's not going anywhere. The wound looks good, but between the starvation and the loss of muscle, Alvin won't be able to move anytime soon. You could kill him if you tried to kick him out."

Ronald's expression told Alvin that he was thinking about it. Clearly, he didn't care about Alvin and didn't want him to stick around, but he wasn't the only one making this decision. Alvin had to keep that in mind.

Ronald was only one voice. Alvin might be unable to convince him to give him a chance, but he was sure he could convince Karen and the other woman. He might even be able to convince the rest of the council.

He could hope.

"We can have someone pick him up," Ronald said. "As you pointed out, there are plenty of humans here. They could grab him and take him out of the forest. He wouldn't have to walk."

Arlene's eyes narrowed. "What don't you understand when I tell you that he can't be moved? He can't leave this bed. Or are you going to move the entire bed? Because I think

Roman would have something to say about that."

"He can stay as long as he wants as far as I'm concerned," Roman said quietly. "I trust him not to hurt me."

"How can you?" Ronald asked, looking around the room. "We don't know anything about him. He might have said he's not here to hurt our alphas, but since he's arrived, several of them have been shot at. How can it be a coincidence?"

"Coincidences exist," Arlene said. "But even if he *is* the man who shot at the alphas, he won't shoot anyone anytime soon. He's not moving from this bed."

"I'm fine with that," the third woman interjected.

"Of course you are," Ronald grumbled. "These are your people. Your alpha probably asked you to agree."

The woman arched a brow. "Are you telling me I'm allowing my alpha to influence me and my decisions? Because council members don't work like that, or at least, I don't. I don't know how it works with the bats, but Jasper would never try to force me into making a decision I'm not comfortable with."

"That's not what I was saying, Olga," Ronald said quickly.

"Good." Olga looked at Alvin. "As far as I'm concerned, you're allowed to stay as long as you need to heal. Roman will keep an eye on you, but remember, I won't be making the final decision on my own. Ronald, Karen, and I are only three members of the council. Other members will want to see you and might make a different decision."

Alvin nodded. "I'll deal with the consequences of that when they happen. Thank you." Alvin hoped the other council members would feel the same as Olga, but they might be on Ronald's side, and if they were, it would be a problem.

But it wasn't a problem he needed to deal with now. He looked at Roman, startled to see a smile on the man's face. He'd known Roman didn't want him to go, but he hadn't realized he'd be so happy to have him stay.

Alvin was glad he was allowed to stay. Being here meant he wouldn't have to steal food or scavenge what he could find in the forest. He wouldn't have to learn how to deal with his wounded leg without supplies and wouldn't have to pray it didn't get infected.

For now, he was safe. He didn't know how long it would last, but like he'd told Olga, he'd deal with whatever happened next when it happened.

CHAPTER EIGHT

Alvin had been thinking about his meeting with the three council members a lot across the several days since then. He felt stronger now and had too much time to obsess over their words.

Ronald wanted Alvin out of here, and he wouldn't be the only one. Every word he'd said to Alvin had felt like a threat, and Alvin wondered when he'd be back to act on those threats. Ronald might behave as if he'd go along with whatever the council decided, but Alvin wouldn't put it past him to influence the other council members, especially the ones who hadn't been here to talk to him.

It had been days, but no one had come for him yet. That meant he still had time, but how much time was anyone's guess. If the council decided he didn't belong here, they'd have someone pick him up and drive him out of the forest.

Where would they dump him? Would they only reach the gate? If whoever picked him up was a shifter, they wouldn't be allowed any further. Shifters were to stay in their forests, which was why the fences and gates had been built.

But Arlene had mentioned humans living here, so it would probably be one of them. Alvin had spied on a few of the guards before and always wished he could be like them. If he were, he would have been allowed into the forest without having to sneak in. He would have been paid to protect the people who lived here, and he would have become part of their community.

But he couldn't fight his way out of a wet paper bag, and

he'd had no strength to talk about, even before he'd starved half to death. He'd be a shitty guard, so that option was out.

One of the human guards would have to drag him out of the forest. They could go further than the gate, which meant they'd probably drop Alvin off at one of the small towns in the area. What would he do then? Should he stick around and finish healing or try sneaking back into the forest right away?

Alvin had nothing. The only thing he owned was his backpack, which, thankfully, Roman had found under the tree next to him the other night. There wasn't much inside. Alvin didn't have any money to rent a house, and while he was sure he could find a job close by, what good would it do? It still wouldn't allow him into the forest.

He'd been thinking about it since meeting with the three council members, and he'd come to a conclusion. He'd promised he'd stick around and wait for the council's final choice, but he couldn't. He hadn't tried running since the first day, but he was stronger now. His leg still hurt, but he'd been eating a lot and healing. Even though his leg would be a bitch to deal with, he was sure he could find a way around it. He didn't care if he had to hobble his way into the forest.

He wouldn't allow the council to force him to leave.

He'd been planning his escape. He'd kept an eye on Roman and had learned his routine, so he knew that Roman returned to the house as often as he could every day. He always checked on Alvin between patients and his time with Arlene, and they usually had lunch together. Alvin didn't know if that was because Roman believed he'd try running if he wasn't there or if there was another reason for it, but it didn't matter.

There was no way for Alvin to know when Roman would be coming back during the day. It could take him hours to deal with the patient he was seeing, but it could also take only a handful of minutes. The only long stretch of time Roman spent away from Alvin was during the night.

That was when Alvin would leave. Hopefully, the darkness would help him sneak into the woods without anyone noticing him, even if there were guards around. He couldn't escape from a shifter with a good nose, but he could still try. He doubted there were guards nearby, anyway. Roman would have told him if there had been.

Roman had been vocal about his dislike for Ronald and some of the other council members. He wanted them to make the right decision, which he felt was allowing Alvin to stay permanently. Alvin didn't understand why Roman felt so strongly about this, but he liked it, even though it wouldn't help.

Which was why Alvin was leaving tonight. He and Roman had spent the evening together like always. Roman had brought dinner home, and they'd watched something on TV. Roman always sat on the chair next to Alvin's bed, and while his focus was never on Alvin, Alvin wondered if he still kept an eye on him. He was always aware of where Roman was and what he was doing, especially when he was in the room. It felt almost like Roman was a magnet, and Alvin couldn't look away.

Alvin swallowed. That was in the past. He couldn't focus on Roman when he needed to leave him behind. Thinking about how cute Roman was when he watched TV and remembering how red his cheeks went when he caught Alvin staring at him wouldn't help.

Alvin looked at the door. It was slightly open, which meant he could see that the lights in the rest of the house were off. He'd heard Roman go to bed a few hours earlier, which meant the coast was clear. Alvin finally had the opportunity and the strength to run.

Why didn't he want to?

Alvin shook his head and pushed away the blankets. What he wanted didn't matter. The only thing that did was his freedom and finding a place to call home, and he wouldn't allow anyone to take that away from him, especially not Ronald.

He swung his legs off the bed and put his weight on his good leg. Carefully, he got to his feet. He expected pain, but it never came, not even when he started putting more weight on his bad leg. He stopped before standing only on that one, not wanting to push things too far. He didn't have to be fully healed to leave, which was good because he could feel that his leg was still weak. Part of his calf muscle was gone, and Arlene had told him it was a miracle that he'd still be able to walk. Alvin didn't like the scars, but he was alive, and in the end, that was all that mattered.

He was hesitant as he took his first steps, but realizing he wouldn't fall on his face right away helped. He grabbed his backpack and hobbled toward the bedroom door. He silently opened it wider, then paused to make sure Roman wasn't around.

The house was completely silent. Knowing he wouldn't have this anymore made Alvin's heart ache, but he focused on what he would have instead. He'd soon be free, and while life in the forest wasn't easy, he had more experience now. He was sure he could find a way to make it work without starving or getting himself eaten.

Or at least, he hoped so.

He took a step forward, then another. He didn't remember much of the house, but he'd seen glimpses of it through the door since he'd arrived, so he knew where to go to find the front door. He had to walk through the living room, where Roman was sleeping, so he'd have to be careful.

He was. He was as silent as he could be as he hobbled from the bedroom door toward the front door. The living room was silent, and while Alvin was tempted to check on Roman, he didn't dare. Instead, he walked behind the couch, focusing on the door in front of him. He'd almost reached it, and he could feel his freedom calling out to him.

Until the lights turned on.

Alvin blinked and tried to keep his balance, but the surprise made him jerk back, and with too much weight on his bad leg, he felt it buckle. Thankfully, the wall wasn't far, and Alvin caught himself on it.

He gave himself a few seconds to breathe. He knew what had happened. Roman had caught him trying to sneak out of the house, and he'd have words for Alvin. Alvin didn't want to face him, but he had to and felt he owed it to Roman. The man had been taking care of him since he'd found him in the forest, and Alvin shouldn't have been sneaking out.

But he was, and now he'd have to deal with the consequences of it.

Roman waited for Alvin to turn around. He'd known Alvin was up to something over the past few days, and it hadn't been hard to understand what that something was.

Roman could understand why Alvin felt he needed to run, even though he disagreed with that decision. After meeting with the council members, Alvin had freaked out, and while he'd been good at hiding it, he hadn't been good enough. Roman had deduced Alvin's need to run right away, and he'd expected Alvin to do something about it.

That was why he'd stayed awake for hours after going to bed over the past few days. It meant he was exhausted, but it didn't matter anymore.

"Where do you think you're going?" he asked.

Alvin took a few seconds to turn to face Roman. His sheepish expression almost made Roman smile, but it was the only thing to smile about in this situation. Either Alvin didn't understand how badly he could have hurt himself, or he did understand and didn't care.

Did he want to be free that badly? Roman could never understand that. He'd always had a home, even though he'd disliked it for most of his life. He'd always known he had a place here, but Alvin had been alone for most of his life, and to counteract that, he'd tried finding a home. He'd been convinced he could find one here, and while Roman hoped he would, he didn't think that living alone in the forest was what Alvin was aiming for.

"You're awake," Alvin said.

Roman rolled his eyes. "I am. Will you tell me what you were doing?"

Alvin sighed and leaned heavily against the wall. "Why do you ask? You already know what I was doing."

"You were running," Roman murmured.

Alvin nodded and closed his eyes. "I felt it was the only thing I could do, and I still feel that way. We both know that Ronald wants me out of the forest, and while I don't know him as well as you do, I wouldn't put it past him to influence the other council members. Hell, I wouldn't put it past him to force them into making the same decision he has. He feels like the kind of person who can do that."

"He *is* that kind of person," Roman confirmed as he moved closer. "And I understand why you ran. Maybe I would've done the same in your place. You have to think before you do these things, though."

Alvin looked at Roman. "You think I haven't thought about it?"

"I know you have, but you have to realize just how badly you were wounded. You can't just waltz out of this place and start living in the forest again. You won't find enough food, and even though I see you have your backpack, I doubt you have enough antibiotics and painkillers in there. Once you'd taken all of them, what would you have done? And what would you have done about food? You didn't stop by the kitchen to grab any, but even if you had, it wouldn't have lasted forever."

"I had to try. I know you don't understand, but this is my home, even though I'm not a shifter. I won't let anyone take it away from me."

Roman moved even closer and put a hand on Alvin's arm. Alvin jerked back but didn't shake Roman's hand off, so Roman decided to leave it there.

"You have to have faith in Jasper," he said. "He's doing everything he can to ensure you're allowed to stay."

"How can I have faith in him when I don't know him? How can I trust that he's doing what I want? Even if he is, how can I be sure the council will lean his way?"

Roman understood where Alvin was coming from, and he wasn't wrong. There was no way to know the council's decision, and Roman couldn't reassure Alvin on that. He didn't know the council members well except for Olga. He could already tell that at least one of them wouldn't want Alvin to stay, and as Alvin had pointed out, Ronald was probably the kind of person who could influence others quite easily.

"Okay, so if you can't have faith in Jasper, how about you have faith in me?" he asked. "I can promise that whatever the council decides, you'll always have a place here with me. If it comes to it, I'll help you run away and provide you with food and whatever you might need."

Alvin's eyes went wide. "You'd do that for me?"

Roman nodded. "I believe your place is here with us, and it doesn't matter that you can't shift. We've allowed an entire family to move here, even though they're human and have never been able to shift into foxes. Like you, they have shifters in their family tree, which is why they were allowed to move here. The only difference between you and them is the way you ended up in the forest, and I don't feel that should be enough reason to kick you out. You deserve to be here just as much as Dean and his family do. I'm sure the council will see that."

"What if they don't?" Alvin whispered.

"If they don't, we'll fight them. We won't be the only ones, either. Jasper will fight for you, as will Dean. You're not alone anymore, Alvin. You never have to be alone anymore unless that's what you want." And Roman didn't think it was.

That was why Alvin was here, after all. He wanted a place to call home and probably a family. He wanted to be with people who understood him and would welcome him with open arms. He might not have found it right away, but he had now, and Roman was ready to fight for him to keep it.

He didn't know why this was so important to him, but he'd seen enough death and fear. He didn't want to lose anyone else, not even a human he barely knew.

He didn't want to lose *Alvin*, and he'd fight as hard as he could to ensure he didn't.

CHAPTER NINE

It had been a few days since Alvin had attempted his last run for freedom, and Roman was relieved that he hadn't tried again. He didn't know if that meant Alvin had believed him when he'd promised to support him and do anything he could to ensure that Alvin was allowed to stick around, but even if he didn't, he wasn't running, and that was what mattered. He was facing this head-on and allowing his body to heal, which was what Roman had wanted.

He hoped he wouldn't regret it.

He peeked sideways at Alvin, who was sitting next to him on the couch. They'd started doing that over the past few days, and Roman liked it. He liked that Alvin clearly felt he could relax next to him. He liked that they fit together as if they both belonged on this couch.

Maybe they did. It was hard to imagine a life without Alvin anymore. He was part of Roman's life, and Roman didn't want to lose him.

He prayed he wouldn't and hadn't lied when he'd told Alvin that everything would be all right.

Alvin needed time to heal, but more than that, Roman wanted him to feel like he belonged there. No one would run unless they absolutely had to, and it wasn't right for anyone to try to kick Alvin out. He might have snuck into the forest, but as far as Roman was concerned, Alvin was here to stay. He wouldn't mind a roommate, and he'd mention that to anyone who asked.

But it was weird to have Alvin around. Roman had lived

alone since leaving his parents' house at eighteen, and while it had been easy to ignore that Alvin was there while he'd been stuck in the bedroom, it wasn't anymore. Alvin was everywhere Roman looked, and while getting used to that took some time, Roman had to admit he liked it.

He enjoyed coming home at night to find someone waiting for him. He didn't need Alvin to cook or clean. He just needed him to be there, resting and healing and not trying to sneak out while he wasn't home.

"You keep looking at me," Alvin said.

Roman blinked and realized that he was staring. He didn't know for how long, but he quickly looked away, unsure how to take it or how Alvin would take it. "Sorry."

Alvin smiled. "It's fine. I can tell you were thinking hard about something."

"I was thinking about you, actually."

Alvin looked surprised. "You were?"

"It's good to see you finally accepted that you need time to rest."

Alvin softly snorted. "It's more that I've accepted that people know who and where I am. Even if I were to run, I'm sure the council could find me. Now that they know who they're looking for, it would be easier than before."

Unfortunately, he was right. If it came to it and Alvin had to run back into the forest, it would be hard for him to hide the way he had the first time around. Roman still wasn't a hundred percent sure how Alvin had managed it. Maybe he'd had enough time to get deeper into the forest after crawling through the hole. He'd smelled pretty ripe when Roman had found him, and that was all a shifter would have been able to smell. They would have thought he was an animal or something like that.

But not anymore. Now people knew he was here, so they'd know where to look if he ran. Alvin wouldn't be going far anyway with a leg that was still healing, and while Roman was glad that Alvin hadn't tried running again, he didn't like the thought of what would happen if Ronald had things his way.

Alvin surprised Roman by knocking their shoulders together. "I'll be fine," he said as if he was trying to reassure Roman, even though it should be the other way around. "Even if I can't convince the council to let me stay, I'll find a way back in. I'll be smarter about it the next time around, and they won't see me coming."

Roman was pretty sure they would, but he didn't want the smile on Alvin's lips to vanish. If Alvin wanted to believe this was what would happen, then Roman wouldn't try to convince him otherwise.

Alvin was allowed to dream, at least for a while. Roman was, too. It was just weird that his dreams involved him and Alvin sitting on the couch together at the end of the day.

"I kind of hate that you're here because you've given up," he told Alvin.

"I haven't given up. I just know that this time, running won't help me."

"I wish you'd feel like you belonged here."

"I wish the same, but for now, this is the way things are. This isn't my home just yet."

Maybe it was because Alvin never saw anyone except Roman and Arlene. He'd met Jasper, but the alpha hadn't stuck around for long, and Alvin hadn't seen him again since. Would it make him feel better if he met Jasper again? Maybe Dean could be there this time. He was in the same position as Alvin, after all. He was human but had shifter ancestry, so he'd know how Alvin felt.

But Dean had been allowed to stay, and Alvin might not. Roman wouldn't want Alvin to resent Dean, especially because he hoped that if Alvin was allowed to stay, he could become a surfeit member. Dean might enjoy having someone in a similar position close by, and Jasper had seemed to like Alvin well enough when they'd talked. Alvin was already in surfeit territory, but even more importantly, Roman *wanted* him to stay.

He didn't want to lose Alvin, to the human world or to another territory. He wanted Alvin to feel at home with the surfeit, and he felt like the only way to make that happen was to show him how good a home it could be. It would have been impossible if Silas had still been in charge, but he wasn't. Jasper was, and Roman was sure he'd agree to have Alvin stick around if he could.

Maybe all of this would hurt Alvin more if he was forced to leave, but Roman wanted him to feel like this was his home in case he could stay. That meant he needed to leave the house and get to know people beyond Roman.

Roman would have to find a way to make that happen. He wanted Alvin to be happy, and while there was nothing he could do about the council and their decision, he could change the rest of Alvin's life for the better.

Alvin liked this. When he'd snuck into the forest, hell, when he'd first arrived at Roman's house, he could never have imagined he and Roman would end up sitting together on the couch watching TV. It felt familiar already, and Alvin liked the thought of doing it for years to come.

He liked *Roman*.

He didn't know what it meant or what would happen, but he was frightened. What if he was forced to leave Roman? What if these were the only peaceful days he had left? If the council decided he had to leave, he wouldn't be able to argue. He might not be allowed to talk to them to convince them that he needed to stay.

The situation was too precarious for him to try anything with Roman, but at the same time, what if he was allowed to stay? Was that something Roman would want to continue doing?

Roman's phone vibrated on the coffee table. He quickly grabbed it, and Alvin knew what was happening from his expression. It wasn't the first time a patient called Roman during the evening, and it was usually bad when someone felt ill enough to call him this late.

"Hello?" Rowan answered.

Alvin couldn't hear the other side of the conversation, but Roman's expression was grim, so he wasn't surprised when Roman turned to him after hanging up.

"Go," Alvin said.

"Are you sure? I could call Arlene."

"Why should you? These are your people, not hers. They called you for a reason, and I won't keep you from them."

Roman was still hesitant, but eventually, he nodded. "I'll have my phone with me, so if anything happens, call me."

"I promise I will, but don't worry about me. I'll be fine."

"And please, don't try to run."

Alvin grinned. "I'm past that. I'm not going anywhere unless you kick me out."

Roman reached out and squeezed Alvin's hand. "That's never going to happen."

"I guess that means I finally found a home, then."

This conversation was too important to have right before Roman left for work, but Alvin wanted him to know that he understood what Roman was saying, both with his words and with his gestures. Roman wanted Alvin to feel at home here, and he did.

Alvin just hoped no one would take it away from him.

Even though it was clear they both wanted to talk, Roman had work to do. He quickly went to his bedroom to change, then grabbed his backpack, and after a moment of hesitation at the door, waved at Alvin and disappeared into the night. For a moment after the door closed, Alvin stayed where he was, pondering his options. It wasn't late, and he didn't want to go to bed yet. He'd spent too much time in that bedroom while he'd been healing, and the less he saw it now, the better he felt.

He wasn't really keen on watching TV without Roman by his side, but it was better than nothing, and the noise helped distract him.

He was just getting back into the movie when someone knocked on the door. Alvin quickly paused the movie and got to his feet, but once he was standing up, he hesitated. He could hobble to the front door, but it was still a bit awkward for him to walk around, and he had no idea who was there. "Yes?" he called out.

There was a moment of silence, then the door opened. Alvin tensed, not knowing what to expect.

A guy peeked in. Alvin had no idea who he was, and he frowned, wondering what the guy was doing there. He didn't hesitate to walk into the house, almost as if he'd already been there.

The guy noticed Alvin standing there like an idiot and smiled. "Hi. I'm Dean."

Dean had dark red hair, brown eyes, a lot of freckles, and looked like he'd swallowed a small melon. Alvin cocked his head, wondering if he was seeing that right, but there was no denying it.

Maybe Dean was a big drinker, although now that Alvin knew the man's name, he was sure that wasn't so. Dean was the alpha mate. Alvin had never met him, but he'd heard enough about him from Roman.

Dean sighed. "You can ask if you want. Everyone does, especially when they're not used to this kind of situation."

"What kind of situation? And I'm sorry, but Roman isn't here. He had to visit a patient."

Dean nodded and moved forward. Alvin watched him come closer, wondering what was happening.

"I know. He called me and told me he had to see a patient and that he'd left you alone in the house." Dean flopped onto the couch and pressed a hand against his stomach.

Alvin couldn't make sense of this. His brain kept telling him one thing, but it was impossible.

He slowly sat back down but didn't put the movie back on. He was more interested in Dean. "So Roman asked you to play babysitter?" he asked.

Dean snickered. "Not really, although I wouldn't put it past him, considering you've tried running a few times. But no, he just told me he had to leave, and I decided to visit. Jasper's out, too, and I was bored. I'm never allowed to do anything these days."

Dean said that while rubbing his stomach again, and Alvin decided he *had* to ask. Would it be rude? *Definitely.* That wouldn't stop Alvin from asking.

"I don't want to be rude," he started.

"But you want to know why I look pregnant."

"Yes. I'm sorry, but it's just odd. It shouldn't be possible."

"It wouldn't be if I were completely human, but I'm like you. I have shifters in my family tree, and because of that, I got pregnant." He gestured at his stomach. "I just wish we'd found out sooner. I wouldn't be in this situation if we had. I don't think I'm ready to be a dad, but there's no getting out of it."

Alvin stared as his brain tried to make sense of what Dean had said. He was human, but he had shifters in his family tree. Those shifters meant that he was able to get pregnant.

Dean was pregnant. He was a man, and he was pregnant.

"Are you a trans man?" Alvin blurted out, even though he

knew he shouldn't be that nosy.

"Nope. I was born a man, and I still am. I just seem to have bits and pieces that normal human guys don't have."

Suddenly, Alvin could see himself with a pregnant stomach, and the thought was enough to make him panic. "Can *I* get pregnant?"

Dean paused for a moment, then shrugged. "I don't know, and I don't recommend finding out by getting pregnant."

"I don't want children. I mean, maybe in the future, but not right now."

Dean arched a brow. "Are you having unprotected sex?"

Alvin quickly shook his head. "No sex."

"Then I don't see the problem. This happened because Jasper and I didn't know any better. Since he's a shifter, we didn't use protection, but we should have. Just make sure that if you have sex with anyone, you use a condom. This thing isn't something you can be sure of until the healers get their hands on you. If you want to know, you should ask Roman and Arlene. They'll be able to tell you."

Alvin swallowed. "Can Roman get pregnant?" Dean had mentioned it had something to do with having shifter DNA, so it was possible.

"Not as far as I know. Only some shifter men can get pregnant. They're called carriers, and there are many in the forest, so don't be surprised if you see pregnant men around. Compared to the number of normal shifter guys, though, they're a small group. You probably won't be able to get pregnant, so I wouldn't worry too much if I were you. This was just my luck, but it would be too big of a coincidence if it happened to you, too."

Alvin had many questions but didn't want to abuse Dean's patience. Besides, Dean looked tired, and considering he was the alpha mate, it was better if Alvin took a step back.

It didn't look like Dean knew much more than he did,

anyway. If Alvin wanted answers, he'd have to ask the people who knew more about all of this.

When was Roman coming home?

Roman was exhausted but relieved by the time he parked his car in front of the house. He'd been worried when he'd gotten the call, but Mr. Wallace would be fine, even though he needed rest. He was one of the oldest skunks in the surfeit, and while Roman knew that eventually he'd pass away, he wasn't ready for that to happen today. Thankfully, it wouldn't, and Roman felt at peace as he got out of the car. He was home, and he could see there was still a light on in the living room, which meant Alvin was waiting for him. It wasn't that late, but Alvin needed rest, and Roman found himself frowning as he pushed open the door.

"What are you still doing awake?" he asked.

Alvin jumped to his feet. His expression told Roman he'd been caught doing something he shouldn't be doing, but Roman couldn't see anything odd. Alvin had just been on the couch watching TV.

"How's your patient?" Alvin asked.

Roman stepped inside and closed the door. "He'll be fine."

"Good. Can I get pregnant?"

Roman blinked. "Where's that question coming from?"

Alvin started pacing, or rather, he tried to pace. He walked with a limp, though, so he hobbled and had to catch himself on the back of the couch. Roman wanted to tell him to sit down, but he could see Alvin was agitated and didn't want to dismiss his feelings.

"I had someone visit me tonight after you called your alpha mate to tell him I'd be alone."

Roman frowned. "I did call him. I wanted him and Jasper to know I'd gotten a call and would be with a patient."

"You didn't ask Dean to babysit me?"

"No."

"So you trust I'm not going to run?"

Roman hesitated. "I have no doubt that you'll try again if you're not allowed to stay, but not right now. You promised you wouldn't, and I trust you."

Alvin stared at Roman with wide eyes. "You trust me?"

Roman was exhausted, but this conversation seemed important to Alvin. He wasn't sure what part of the conversation mattered the most, but he'd take things one at a time. "Of course I trust you. Why shouldn't I?"

"Maybe because I tried to run twice? Or it could be because I snuck in through a hole in the fence instead of coming here through the right procedures."

Roman dumped his bag by the door and took his shoes off. "And what are the correct procedures? Because as far as I know, there aren't any. Dean's family was allowed to move because he works for the government. You wouldn't have had a way to be authorized to move here, so you did it the only way you could think of. As for you running, it doesn't matter. You told me you wouldn't, and I trust that you won't."

Roman flopped onto the couch and stretched out his legs. He closed his eyes, but only briefly, because he wanted to know what was happening with Alvin. He felt Alvin sit next to him, and they were both silent for a moment.

Roman remembered Alvin's other question, so he looked at him. "As for you getting pregnant, I don't know. I'd have to examine your blood to be sure. I should have told you about Dean's condition but didn't think of it. For me, it's fairly normal to see a pregnant man. It's not as common as pregnant women, but it does happen."

Alvin was a little pale, but nothing that worried Roman. He looked overwhelmed, though, which Roman wished he could help him with. Unfortunately, Alvin would need to deal with this for himself. Roman understood he was stunned and couldn't quite believe that some men could get pregnant, but he'd seen the proof.

"I'm not used to men being pregnant," Alvin said. "Well, they sometimes are, but we're talking about trans men. Dean said that's not what he is."

"He has shifter DNA, like you, and for him, it means being able to get pregnant. It's not that common, so you probably don't have to worry about it, but if you want to be sure, I can check."

"Yes, please. If I can get pregnant, I want to know."

Roman hadn't thought of checking sooner. It was fairly rare even in shifters, so Dean had been a surprise for everyone. He was an outlier, and Roman didn't expect Alvin to be like him, but if it helped Alvin feel better, he didn't have a problem testing him. Normally, he could tell by scent, but he couldn't with Dean. The alpha mate just smelled human, as did Alvin.

Alvin relaxed as if Roman telling him he'd test him helped. "I mean, don't get me wrong, I think I'll want children eventually, but not right now. Everything's a mess, and I'm not even sure I'll be allowed to stay. Can you imagine what would happen if they kicked me out and I was pregnant? People wouldn't know what to make of me, and I don't think any doctor in the human world would know how to deal with me."

Roman wanted to ask who Alvin was planning on having sex with since he was thinking about this, but he didn't dare. Instead, he patted Alvin's knee. "I'll test you tomorrow. As long as you don't have unprotected sex tonight, you'll be fine."

Alvin's cheeks flushed, and he glanced sideways. "I don't think I will."

Roman wanted to offer himself up, but he didn't. He was

pretty sure Alvin liked him, and he liked Alvin, but Alvin's emotions were all over the place. Would it be right for Roman to offer this? No matter how much Roman wanted to, it would be better if Alvin took the first step. Maybe he would, and maybe he wouldn't. Roman wouldn't be surprised by either of those possibilities. Alvin didn't know what his future would be like, and it would make sense for him to keep his distance. That way, it wouldn't hurt as much if they were separated.

But maybe they wouldn't be. Maybe he and Alvin would have the opportunity to see where things could go between them, and if they did, Roman wanted it to happen. It was still better to let Alvin make the next move, though. Roman was pretty sure he'd been obvious and that Alvin at least suspected he liked him, so the ball was in Alvin's court. Maybe he wouldn't do anything with it, or maybe he'd take charge and do what they both wanted him to do.

But not tonight. Alvin was still worried about being able to get pregnant. For his peace of mind, it would be better if Roman kept his distance.

So instead of kissing Alvin like Roman wanted, Roman leaned closer until their shoulders touched. He grabbed the remote from the side of the couch and turned the movie back on, and they relaxed together.

Roman was keenly aware of Alvin's presence next to him, but he did his best to focus on the screen. Whatever would happen between them, he wasn't in a rush. He wanted to give Alvin pretty much anything, and right now, Alvin needed time.

Roman prayed they'd have it.

CHAPTER TEN

Alvin and Roman had a routine by now. Alvin felt like he'd lived with Roman for a long time rather than just a few weeks, and he liked it, but it also made him nervous. He'd been here for a while, which meant that the council would make their decision about him sooner rather than later. He'd been allowed to stay for the time he needed to heal, but he could walk again, and he could be moved.

He expected the council to come back into his life at any moment. Nothing good would come out of it when they did. Roman's test had shown that Alvin wasn't a carrier, so he wasn't precious to the shifters in the forest. Every time Roman's phone rang, Alvin jumped. When someone knocked on Roman's door, Alvin wanted to hide. Luckily, it didn't happen often, but it did happen, and Alvin loathed feeling so anxious. He wanted to relax in his home, but he couldn't. He wouldn't be able to as long as he didn't know what was expected of him and what had been decided.

When Roman's phone rang, Alvin expected it to be another patient. Roman frowned when he looked at the screen before answering, and Alvin suspected he was the reason Roman mentioned Jasper's name as soon as he did. If Alvin knew who it was, he wouldn't be so jumpy.

"Jasper. Is everything all right?" Roman asked.

Alvin relaxed, but he shouldn't have. Roman's expression grew alarmed, and he stepped away from the stove where he'd been cooking lunch.

"How many?"

This was it, wasn't it? The council was here to kick Alvin out.

Roman turned off the stove and rushed to the window. "What are they doing here? They know the rules. Any of them would have been pissed if you'd done something like this. Don't they understand what they're doing? The council might not care, but they have no right to be here."

Roman's words made Alvin frown. He'd thought Roman was talking about the council, but it didn't sound like they were coming for Alvin. If it wasn't, who was it? Alvin hadn't seen anyone else since he'd arrived here. He'd talked to Dean and Jasper and Arlene, but beyond the three council members who'd visited him initially, that was it. Who would want to see him so badly? It sounded like they were doing something that might be illegal or, even if legal, wasn't accepted. It didn't make sense.

"Yeah, they're here. I'm going to hang up and open the door."

Alvin took a step forward because he didn't want Roman to put himself in danger. Thankfully, it looked like he wasn't the only one because Roman paused. He huffed, then lowered his phone and tapped something on the screen. "You're on speaker," he told Jasper. "And I really doubt they're going to attack me. They're here for Alvin."

"I agree that they are, but it doesn't mean they'll take it nicely when you tell them to fuck off," Jasper said.

It sounded like he was moving quickly, probably on his way here.

"Not only are they invading a territory that isn't theirs, but they're bothering me at my home. They have no right to be here, and if they try anything, I'll make sure to remind them of that."

"Don't do anything stupid," Jasper warned. "I'm coming. I just need you to keep an eye on them and Alvin. I don't want anything to happen to him or you."

Alvin agreed, but he already knew he couldn't stop Roman from doing whatever he wanted. Roman wasn't the kind of person who allowed anyone to intimidate him, maybe because of everything he'd lived through. He hadn't gone into details, but Alvin had gathered that the old alpha hadn't been a great man. Jasper was young and inexperienced, but the few times Alvin had seen him, he could tell that Jasper was doing everything in his power to do a good job. That was what mattered.

Roman set his phone in the bowl on the small table by the door where he left his keys, straightened his back, and opened his door just as someone was about to knock. The man standing on the porch quickly lowered his fist and took a step back. Roman crossed his arms over his chest and glared. "What are you doing here? This isn't your territory, and Jasper assured me he hasn't allowed you to enter."

"We're here for the human," the man said gruffly.

"I don't care why you're here. You have no place in skunk territory unless Jasper allows you in, and he hasn't."

"We just want to see the human," a woman said. "We're worried. Our council members told us he's here, and Ronald mentioned he's dangerous."

Roman snorted. "Hardly. He's still healing, and even though he can walk more easily now, he's not running around the forest attacking people. He's not the shooter, Lindsay."

"We don't know that," the first man said.

Roman turned his glare back to him. "You would if you listened. This isn't your place, Alpha Foley. Jasper hasn't allowed you to come into our territory, and we both know what you'd do if he'd done something like this. He's not looking to start a war with the bats, but you better turn around and go home."

"Just let us meet him," a second man said. "If you're so sure he's not dangerous, it won't hurt anyone."

"It might hurt *him*. I'm not letting you in my house. Jasper is coming. He'll deal with you when he arrives."

"There are three of us and only one of him," Alpha Foley said.

He was right, and Alvin wondered if this was about to end as badly as he feared. Even if it was Jasper's right to defend himself and his territory, he'd be only one against three.

"And you're willing to start a war just to get a good look at the human?" Roman asked. "Because that's what will happen if you don't leave now. Jasper might only be one person, but he's not without allies. The badgers and the bears are on our side, and they're not the only ones."

"He's right," a strong voice said from the forest.

Alvin was startled to see that Jasper had arrived. He'd expected him to get here by car, even though he hadn't seen many of those since he'd arrived in skunk territory. Roman had one because he needed to visit his patients, but everyone else that Alvin had seen through the windows seemed to walk. Jasper had clearly done the same, and even though he was windswept and wore jeans and a sweater, he looked every bit the alpha he was. He stood up straight, his expression serious but not glaring, as he took in the three alphas on Roman's porch.

"Jasper," Lindsay said. "I apologize for coming here without asking for your permission, but we need to talk to the human. There's been another shooting."

Alvin didn't know Jasper well, so he couldn't be sure of how the alpha reacted to the news. It didn't look like he did at all, but he nodded at Lindsey. "I'm aware."

"The deer alpha isn't dead, but it was close."

"I'm sorry to hear that, but I don't understand why that gave you the right to barge into my territory without talking to me."

"It has to have been the human," Alpha Foley said as he pushed Lindsay to the side to face Jasper.

He was rude, just like Ronald. From what Alvin remembered, Ronald was a bat shifter, and it seemed that Foley was one, too. Were all bat shifters rude?

"Why would you think that?" Jasper asked.

"He came in when the shootings started. He's still here, and the shootings are still happening. Who else could it be?"

"I don't know who it is," Roman said. "But it's not Alvin. He's wounded, and he can't move quickly."

Alpha Foley turned his glare to Roman. "Looks to me like he's moving just fine."

Alvin was wearing shorts, so Foley could see the bandages around his calf. He couldn't see the extent of the wound, so he might think it was fake. Alvin was ready to tear off the bandages to show him, but thankfully, he didn't have to. Roman had everything in hand.

"He's missing a part of his calf muscle," Roman snapped. "A coyote shifter tore into it. Alvin might be on his feet, but it doesn't mean he can move easily. He has a limp, and until he builds back his calf muscle, he's going to continue limping. Do you really think he could have gone into the forest and shot at an alpha in this condition? What happened when Alpha Garrison was shot? Did someone go after the shooter?"

"They did," the second man answered. "They couldn't find anything."

"Alvin would have still been there, hobbling around. It wasn't him. We were both home together this morning, so I would have known if he'd left the house, and like I said, he can't move. You need to stop focusing on him and find the actual shooter."

Alpha Foley was clearly pissed, but Alvin wasn't too worried. Jasper was there, and he looked ready to tear the man's head off if he as much as breathed too hard in Alvin and

Roman's direction.

Alvin didn't want to start a war but was glad to have Jasper on his side.

Roman was pissed. How dare these alphas come into skunk territory and attack Alvin like this? How dare they demand an explanation without going through Jasper?

Jasper was the alpha, and Alvin was his responsibility right now. If these alphas wanted to know anything about him or to interrogate him, they had to go through Jasper.

Roman wasn't surprised they hadn't. He'd expected better from Lindsay, who'd taken over the porcupine prickle after her father had died, so he was disappointed, but Foley's presence wasn't a surprise. The alpha was a thorn in everyone's side, and while he wasn't as bad as Silas had been, Roman suspected it wasn't because he didn't want to be. He seemed to enjoy power and holding his alpha-ness over everyone as much as Silas had.

"You have your explanation," Jasper said. "Unless there's anything else, you need to leave."

"We're not leaving without him," Foley said, pointing a finger at Alvin, who stood behind Roman.

"He's a member of my surfeit. I won't allow you to take him anywhere, especially when you have no right to be here."

Roman was startled by the conviction in Jasper's voice. Alvin wasn't actually a surfeit member yet, although Roman hoped that one day he would be. He'd have to be allowed to stay in the forest first, though.

"The council hasn't made their decision," Mark Russo, the raccoon alpha, said.

"Maybe not, but I consider him one of mine until they tell me he needs to leave. If you wanted answers from him, you should have gone through me. You shouldn't have barged into my territory without calling me first." Jasper looked at Foley. "Imagine if I'd done the same. How would you have taken it?"

Foley growled, but thankfully, he wasn't stupid enough to attack Jasper. "We want answers," he snapped. "Someone almost died, and one of us might be next. I won't allow anyone to threaten me, especially not a human."

"Alvin hasn't threatened you. You heard Roman. Alvin hasn't left the house, and even if he had, he wouldn't be capable of killing anyone. He can't move fast enough to escape a bunch of shifters who want revenge for their alpha. Unless you have something else to say, you need to leave before I call the council and tell them what you've done."

Foley looked like he wanted to continue arguing and maybe even take things further, but Lindsay put a hand on his arm. She looked at Jasper, and while Roman had been disappointed to see her there, he was glad for her presence. It meant that Jasper would have someone on his side if things went too far.

"We're leaving," she said. "We believe you and your healer, and we shouldn't have entered your territory without permission. We apologize for that."

Foley opened his mouth.

Roman wouldn't have been surprised if he said he wasn't sorry, but one glare from Lindsay made him snap his mouth shut. It was a surprise. Roman didn't want a fight to start on his porch, especially with Jasper's position still somewhat precarious. He'd only been the skunk alpha for a short time, and while the skunks had accepted him, he was still learning. He didn't have anywhere near as much experience as Foley, which probably was why Foley had thought it would be fine for him to enter skunk territory without letting anyone know.

Lindsay dragged Foley toward the car they'd arrived in. The raccoon alpha went willingly, not once looking back.

Roman didn't breathe easier until the car was gone from sight, but even then, he knew it wasn't over.

Jasper had his phone by his ear, and from listening to the conversation, Roman realized he was keeping in touch with the guards. As soon as the car left skunk territory, Roman saw Jasper visibly relaxed.

"They're gone," Jasper said when he hung up.

"I'm really sorry about this," Alvin said.

"Why are you apologizing?" Jasper asked him as he put away his phone. "You have no fault. You didn't shoot the deer alpha and didn't force Foley and the other two to come here and demand an explanation they could have had if they'd called me."

"But it's my fault they were here. They wanted to see me."

"It was still their actions that created a problem, not yours. Don't take that guilt on, Alvin. You had nothing to do with this." Jasper looked at Roman. "Shall we go inside? I have some information about what happened earlier."

Roman quickly stepped aside to let Jasper in. He was glad to be able to close the door. It made him feel safer, even though it was only a piece of wood.

The three of them went to sit in the living room, and like always, Roman chose a spot next to Alvin. Jasper's eyebrows shot up on his forehead, but he didn't ask what was happening. Roman was glad. He didn't know what was happening. He just knew he wanted to be close to Alvin and comfort him.

"I got news of that shooting," Jasper explained. "Alpha Garrison, the deer alpha, was shot just outside his territory an hour ago. As you can imagine, everything has been a mess since then. I expected someone to react like the three alphas who came here did, but I didn't expect them to be so brash as to come into our territory without calling me first. I should have, and I'm sorry they reached your house, Roman."

Roman shook his head. "Just like it wasn't Alvin's fault, it wasn't yours, either."

Jasper smiled. "You're right. Anyway, it's over now. I don't like that they felt so sure of themselves and so convinced I wouldn't do anything, but I'll deal with it. It's not your problem, so don't worry about it."

Roman wondered how he was supposed to not worry about it. He hadn't been surprised to see Foley here, and even Russo made sense, but Lindsay? Everyone had thought she would be a better alpha than her father when she'd taken his place, but now, Roman wondered.

The forest was only just starting to heal from what the old alphas had done. They couldn't afford this kind of behavior, and he truly hoped it wasn't an indication of what was to come. He had faith in Jasper, but Jasper was only one man. What was he supposed to do against a group of alphas who had no faith in him? He had allies, but would they be enough to keep the surfeit safe and protect Alvin?

It was clear that neither Jasper nor Roman thought that Alvin had anything to do with this latest shooting or the others, but Alvin still felt the need to tell them. He cleared his throat, getting the attention of both men.

"I didn't shoot anyone. I didn't even know there had been any shootings. Roman didn't tell me, and between the time I spent in the forest and the time I spent here, I've been out of the loop. I swear I didn't hurt anyone. I never even *wanted* to hurt anyone."

Jasper nodded. "I didn't expect you to be responsible for any of this. Initially, we thought you might be because we had no idea who you were and what you were doing here, but not anymore. You don't have to worry about convincing me."

Roman nodded. "I'm pretty sure Harvey and Silas are behind all of this."

Alvin didn't have to be told who these two men were. He'd never forget Harvey after what he and the guys he'd been talking to in the forest had done, and Alvin heard the name Silas plenty of times since he'd arrived in surfeit territory. He knew Silas was Jasper's father, had been the alpha before him, and wasn't a good person.

"You think my father has something to do with this?" Jasper asked.

He sounded hopeful, but Alvin wasn't, and after hesitating one moment, Roman shook his head.

"I wish I could say I don't, but we both know he has to be involved. This is just like him. He's trying to kill his rivals and the people he feels worked against him. I might not have seen him recently, but I remember him all too well. He has to be pissed that he's in jail and feel betrayed by you and his allies. He'll want revenge, and while he can't do much on his own since he's behind bars, Harvey is still out there. We know they're planning to break your father out of his cell. It wouldn't be a stretch to think that they're also planning to kill as many alphas as possible."

"What would they gain from that?" Alvin asked.

"Power and control," Jasper said in a grim tone. "My father was arrested because alphas stood up to him, and the council finally did what they were created to do. If those people aren't there anymore, it'll be easier for him to regain his power once he breaks out of jail."

Alvin disliked how Jasper talked about that as if it was a given. "Maybe he won't be able to break out of jail."

"We can hope, but I know my father. When he wants something, he gets it, especially when he's angry. I haven't seen him in a while, but he's got to be pissed."

Angry men were dangerous. This didn't bode well for the shifters in the forest, but especially for the skunks.

If the situation had been different, Alvin would have

wanted to leave. He'd snuck into the forest because he wanted a place to call home and be safe where he belonged, but he was in danger here. He didn't have to ask to know what Silas would do to him if he became the alpha again, and the thought made him shiver in horror.

He was selfish. If Silas ever returned, he would kill him, but he'd also kill Jasper and Dean. Even if he didn't kill Dean, Alvin could too easily imagine what might happen to him. Roman had explained that in the past, carriers were treated like incubators, bought and sold and kidnapped, and that the way they'd been treated was one of the reasons things had changed so sharply in recent years. He hadn't gone into details, but he didn't have to.

Alvin didn't want any of that to happen to Dean or anyone else, but it would if Silas took power again.

There was nothing Alvin could do about it. He was only one man and a human at that. He had no authority, and frankly, he didn't want it. He'd do whatever Jasper asked of him and pray it would be enough, but it might not be.

"I know you're worried," Jasper told Alvin. "We all are, but there's more to it for you. I don't want you to worry about not having a place here, though. As long as I'm the alpha, you do."

Alvin swallowed. He didn't want to believe it in case Jasper changed his mind, but how was he supposed to ignore the alpha's words? "You told those alphas that I was a surfeit member," he murmured.

"I meant it." The conviction was strong in Jasper's voice as he continued, "For a long time, I felt like I didn't have a place here. It sounds ridiculous because I always knew I'd be the alpha after my father died, but he never cared about the surfeit's future or mine. He just wanted what was best for him and was ready to tear down anyone standing in his way. Even after I became the alpha, I felt like I didn't belong here. I didn't know how to guide these people, and honestly, I still don't most days, but I'm making my own place here. It's not what my father's place was, but I don't want it to be. I'm not him. That's a good thing, but my new role still feels odd, just like yours feels odd to you."

Alvin didn't fully understand what Jasper was saying and didn't see how their situations were similar, but he could tell Jasper was being honest. He'd felt like he didn't belong, but now, he did, and he was offering the same to Alvin.

Alvin hoped he'd find a place here, too.

He wanted to put down roots, and it felt like he might finally have the opportunity to do so. He didn't know what the council would decide, and he was scared, but even if they kicked him out, he wasn't giving up. He'd find a way to come back.

His place was here, with Roman.

Alvin looked at his friend. He'd always known Roman could be more than that, but he'd been afraid to take that step. The situation had felt too precarious, and there had been too much pain waiting for them. There still was, but Alvin had enough of holding back. Even if he was forced to leave, he and Roman could be happy for now. Wouldn't that be worth the pain they'd feel once it was over?

And maybe it wouldn't have to be over.

Alvin continued thinking about that as Jasper said good-bye and left. He didn't have a plan in mind or anything like that, but as soon as the door closed behind Jasper, Alvin's entire focus was on Roman. Roman noticed it, and his eyes widened as he stared at Alvin.

"Alvin?"

Alvin's mouth was dry, but he ignored it. "I need to say something."

"What is it?"

"I want to be honest with you. I've tried to ignore how I

feel because we don't know what's going to happen, and I don't want to hurt you, but I think it was the wrong approach. Maybe what we need to focus on isn't the pain we'll feel once this is over but the happiness we can have in the meantime."

Roman licked his lips. "What are you talking about?"

Alvin stepped forward. His legs felt weak, but he was grateful for the fact that he was regaining his balance. It meant he didn't make a fool of himself as he closed in on Roman and crowded him against the wall.

"I think it's fairly obvious that I like you," he murmured. "I can't stop watching you, and I miss you when you're not home. If I had a choice, I'd want to spend my life here with you. I don't know if it'll be possible, but even if it's not, I want at least a chance."

Roman's hands landed on Alvin's hips, silently telling him Roman was okay with this. He wasn't pushing Alvin away. He was pulling him closer until their chests brushed against each other, and Alvin could feel Roman's warmth through their clothes.

"You have one," Roman murmured.

Alvin was glad to hear that because he was done resisting the pull between them. He cupped Roman's cheek with one hand while hooking his other arm around him. Roman came willingly, tilting his face up, and when their lips met, Alvin knew this was the right thing to do.

He'd never felt like he had a home before meeting Roman, but now, he did. Alvin didn't understand how, but *Roman* had become his home, which meant Alvin would need to find a way to be allowed to stay. It wasn't only his happiness at stake but also Roman's, and that was something Alvin was ready to fight for.

CHAPTER ELEVEN

"You have no idea what he wants?"

Alvin shook his head. "You heard our conversation. He didn't tell me."

Alvin was curious. He hadn't expected Jasper to call and request that Alvin come to see him. Alvin had barely left Roman's house since he'd arrived, and when he had, he hadn't got further than the forest surrounding the place. Now, Jasper wanted to see him in his home, and Alvin was nervous.

Part of him wondered if Jasper was about to kick him out. No matter how often Jasper told Alvin he had a place here, it was still hard for Alvin to believe. Maybe it was because he still hadn't heard from the council, or maybe because he'd never had a place to call home, no matter how much he'd yearned for one. Either way, it was easier to believe that something bad was about to happen than to believe something good could come out of this.

Alvin squeezed Roman's hand. He already had something good. Roman had been by his side through all of it, and he wasn't going anywhere. The two of them were together, and while they'd avoided talking about what would happen if the council kicked Alvin out, the rest of their relationship was perfect.

Roman was perfect. He wasn't only handsome but also sweet and gentle, and he was one of the most caring people Alvin had ever met. He seemed to have infinite patience with Alvin and the people he cared for. He was strong and ready to stand up to bullies like he had with those three alphas.

People tended to underestimate him because of how gentle he was.

But not Alvin. He knew all of this, and every single one of the reasons he liked Roman for was also one of the reasons he was falling in love with him. That way probably held heartbreak, but Alvin would deal with it if it happened. In the meantime, he'd already decided to take advantage of the time he and Roman had together.

Which was why he was slightly annoyed with Jasper. He didn't mind talking to the alpha. In fact, he liked him, and he thought they might become friends if they had the opportunity. But Jasper wanting to see Alvin at his home meant that Alvin and Roman had to leave theirs. It gave them less time to spend together alone, and even though Alvin realized that they needed other people in their lives, it also felt like they were running on borrowed time.

"Everything will be okay," Roman reassured Alvin as he squeezed his hand.

"I know."

They were both lying, and they knew it, but it didn't matter. They could lie to each other when it came to this. They were adults and understood it.

"We're there," Roman said a few minutes later as they stepped out from between the trees.

The air was cool, but it wasn't raining, and while Roman had suggested he drive them here, Alvin had wanted to walk. He liked Roman's house and their time alone together, but it had been a long time since he'd stretched his legs.

"How's your leg?" Roman asked.

"It's fine. I promise I'd tell you if it wasn't."

Roman's eyes narrowed. "Would you?"

"No more lies between us."

Roman stared for a moment before nodding and pulling

Alvin along again. "No more lies," he agreed.

The house where Dean and Jasper lived was nice. There were plants on the porch, along with a bench, a few blankets, and several pairs of boots. It looked lived-in, which Alvin thought was delightful.

Roman knocked on the door, and it opened quickly, as if Jasper had been waiting for them. Jasper grinned, which startled Alvin because he didn't think he'd ever seen the alpha smile so widely.

"Come in," Jasper said.

Roman stared at him. "What happened?"

"Nothing. Why would you think something happened?" Jasper quickly asked.

Roman waved a hand at his alpha's face. "Because of that. It's creepy."

Someone laughed behind Jasper, and Alvin wasn't surprised when Dean grabbed his boyfriend's shoulder and pulled him into the house. "Let them in before you jump them," he said fondly.

Jasper caught Dean's waist and pulled him closer to kiss him. Dean's cheeks reddened, but he leaned into the touch. Their love was obvious, making Alvin wonder what he and Roman would look like if they were allowed to have a future together. Would it be like this for them, too?

Well, minus the pregnant belly.

Alvin did his best not to look at it, but he was pretty sure Dean noticed it anyway. He rolled his eyes and waved at Alvin and Roman to come in, which was a relief. Alvin might still be weirded out about the male pregnancy thing, but he wasn't the pregnant one. Dean was. Not only was he the alpha mate, but he was also someone Alvin hoped would become a friend. He didn't want to offend him in any way.

"What's going on, then?" Roman asked as he and Alvin were led to the kitchen.

"You're pretty rude," Jasper complained.

"You're used to me being rude."

Jasper laughed. "I am. I can't believe there was a time you were afraid of me."

Alvin blinked. He found that hard to believe, but it made sense considering what he knew of the surfeit's history. Roman had told him he hadn't always felt comfortable with Jasper as the alpha, mostly because he hadn't known him. He did now, and they were close.

The four of them sat at the table after Jasper got everyone coffee. Dean had tried to do so, but Jasper had glared at him until he'd sat down, rolling his eyes again.

"So I'm sure you're curious about why you're here," Jasper said.

Alvin took a sip of coffee before nodding. "I didn't expect it. It's made me a bit nervous."

"I hope you didn't think I was going to kick you out."

"It did cross my mind, but Roman assured me you wouldn't do that."

Jasper's expression turned more serious. "He's right. I already told you that you're one of us, and I meant it. In fact, that's why you're here."

Jasper and Dean glanced at each other. It looked like they were communicating without words. No matter how hard Alvin tried to understand what they were telling each other with their eyes, he couldn't.

Jasper turned back to Alvin. "We still don't know what the council will decide when it comes to your presence in the forest, but Dean and I decided we didn't care. We guide the surfeit, and if we want you to be a surfeit member, then it's in our right to ask you to become one officially."

Alvin told himself not to hope too much, even though Jasper's words could only have one meaning. "Are you asking me to become a surfeit member?" He knew Jasper had said he was a member when he'd confronted Alpha Foley, but that wasn't official, and they'd never asked him.

"We are," Jasper confirmed.

"Won't that get you in trouble with the council?"

"Probably, but I honestly don't care. If they can't see that you're innocent and deserve to be here as much as Dean does, then what they say doesn't matter to me."

Alvin knew it wasn't that easy. Every alpha had control over their territory, but the council had been created for a reason, and that reason was important. They were there in case the alphas abused their authority, and in some ways, what Jasper was doing could be seen as doing just that. He wasn't doing it to hurt anyone, but Alvin doubted most people would care. Ronald certainly wouldn't.

Alvin wanted to shout that of course he wanted to be a surfeit member, but he had to be sure of what it meant. "What if the council decides to kick me out? What will happen then?"

"We'll fight for you. If you're a surfeit member, it's in my right to demand you be allowed to stay with us. The only reason the council could drag you away is if you've done something that breaks their laws, but you haven't."

"I snuck into the forest."

Jasper grinned. "You did, but I checked the council laws. There's nothing about humans sneaking into the forest through a hole in the fence or otherwise, which means they don't have anything against you. No matter how much Ronald bitches about your presence here, if you're a surfeit member, you have every right to stay."

Alvin hoped Jasper was right. He didn't want to say yes and settle into his new life only to be kicked out by the council.

But even if they did kick him out, in the meantime, he would finally have the life he'd dreamed of. There was no way he could say no to that.

"I don't want to be any trouble for the surfeit, but I can't refuse," he said, grinning like an idiot. "So yes. I want to be an official surfeit member."

As Roman and Alvin walked back to Roman's house, Roman had a hard time wrapping his mind around what had happened. Neither he nor Alvin had expected Jasper to ask Alvin to officially become a surfeit member. It was a dangerous offer that could create all kinds of troubles with the council, but Jasper had made it anyway.

Roman knew why he'd done it. He wanted to protect Alvin, and he'd felt like Alvin was his responsibility even before he'd become a surfeit member. While Roman was relieved that Alvin wouldn't be going anywhere and that he'd have the kind of protection he wouldn't have had if he'd just been a human invader, he was also worried.

What would happen if the council decided to kick Alvin out? Since he was a surfeit member, Jasper would be in his right to stand up for him, and Roman had no doubt he would. That was why he'd asked Alvin to become a surfeit member — to protect him when no one else could.

But it might pull the surfeit into a war they couldn't win. Every territory had to follow some rules, and one of them was accepting the council's laws. If they refused to do so, it would bring back the chaos that had been in the forest before, and that wasn't something anyone wanted. Too many people had been abused and hurt, including Jasper.

But would Jasper follow the council's ruling if he felt it wasn't fair?

"You don't look happy that I became a surfeit member," Alvin said.

His tone told Roman that he was a little hurt, which was understandable. "I am. I want you to stay with the surfeit,"

Roman reassured him.

"But you're worried."

Roman couldn't lie to Alvin. "I am. I want Jasper to protect you, but it could pull the surfeit into a war we can't win. The council has teams they send into various territories when the laws are being broken, and if they rule that you have to leave and Jasper insists you shouldn't, that's what they'll do."

"Do you think I should have said no when he offered me a place here?"

"No. I think you made the right decision, and so did Jasper. It's not you or him I'm worried about, but the council. Hopefully, we have enough allies that the council will rule in your favor, but there's no way to know." And until they made their decision, Roman would be nervous.

He couldn't help it and hoped Alvin wouldn't be offended. This had nothing to do with him and everything to do with the council and the way they held Roman's future in their hands.

It was a bit ridiculous to think like that already, but Roman couldn't imagine his life without Alvin. Alvin had become a part of it and made Roman happy, and he didn't want to lose him.

Alvin squeezed Roman's hand. "I can't promise that everything will be all right, but I'm sure the council will see that the best way to avoid a war is to allow me to stay. I don't think they want infighting any more than you and Jasper do. Besides, I'm not dangerous, and I'm not the person shooting alphas. I'm human, so if something happens, it'll be fairly easy for any shifter to subdue me."

The thought of Alvin doing anything that would lead to that was ridiculous, but their problems weren't over. There was no way to know what the future held, but Roman decided that he couldn't live in fear. Whatever the council decided, Roman wouldn't put his life on pause for them. He would enjoy his time with Alvin, whether it was just the beginning of a long life together or the only few weeks they'd have.

"We should celebrate," he told Alvin as he pulled him forward faster.

"And how do you plan on doing that?"

Roman gave Alvin what he hoped was a wicked smile. He wanted to seduce this man, but he wasn't sure how to do it. He had no experience when it came to dating anyone. "I think you know."

Alvin's expression told Roman he did.

They rushed toward the house. Roman kept an eye on Alvin just in case his leg acted up, but he seemed to be walking easily. He had a limp, and he probably always would, but he could walk, and that was the important thing.

They didn't race each other to the house, but it was a close thing. Roman barged in, already taking off his jacket. He felt all bubbly inside and happier than he'd ever been. He didn't want to think of the possibility that he might lose this. As far as he was concerned, this was how the rest of his life would be. He and Alvin would grow old together, happy in this little house, and that was that. Who cared what the council thought? Roman certainly didn't.

He hopped on one foot as he tried to remove the shoe on the other. He didn't dare look at Alvin in case what he saw flustered him so much that he stopped moving.

He'd already seen Alvin naked when he'd taken care of him while he was wounded, but it wasn't the same thing. Now, they'd both be naked, and Alvin was as healthy as he'd get. Roman would still be careful in the way they moved, but he didn't feel the need to wrap Alvin in a blanket and bundle him into bed.

Not for the reasons he had before, anyway. He did want to get Alvin into bed, but for an entirely different activity.

As soon as Roman's shoes were off, he rushed toward the

bedroom. He was glad his house only had one floor because it meant Alvin was comfortable moving around it. He was slower than Roman, but that was to be expected. It wasn't a problem. It gave Roman more time to get naked and into bed.

He was still wearing his underwear and half of his pants by the time Alvin reached him. He quickly shook his leg, dropped his pants, dove onto the bed, and wriggled under the blankets. Once there, he took a deep breath and pulled down his boxer briefs. He could feel his cheeks were hot, but he ignored it as he dragged his underwear out from under the blankets and threw it at Alvin's head.

Alvin caught it and dumped it on the floor. He'd removed his jacket and sweater, but he was still wearing his jeans, and Roman wanted them off.

He held his hands out and wiggled his fingers. "Come here."

"I am," Alvin assured him.

Roman didn't try to get him to move faster. He didn't want Alvin to hurt himself. Roman didn't want Alvin to feel like he needed more than he could give. Whatever Alvin could give was perfect as far as Roman was concerned.

Even though Roman had already seen Alvin naked, he still looked away when Alvin took off his jeans and boxer briefs. This was a different situation, and Roman was a bit flustered. He didn't know how to deal with the naked man in his bedroom.

But he'd have to learn quickly.

He raised the blankets, and Alvin slid under them. He settled next to Roman as Roman rolled to his side so they could look at each other. For a moment, that was all they did. Roman almost couldn't believe that Alvin was here with him, and he couldn't stop himself from smiling like an idiot.

"I'm not going anywhere," Alvin murmured.

"I know."

They reached for each other at the same time. Roman wiggled forward, hesitating just a second before plastering his body against Alvin's. He hooked a leg around Alvin's waist, careful of Alvin's calf. The last thing they needed was for Alvin to be in pain while they were naked in bed together for the first time.

Luckily, Alvin didn't seem to be experiencing any kind of pain. He grabbed Roman's ass with both hands and hauled him close, taking Roman's breath away. Roman didn't know where to start, but Alvin kissed him, and he decided it was perfect.

Alvin had more experience than Roman, and Roman was happy to let him take the lead. He didn't think Alvin would push him into something he wasn't ready for. They might not have talked about this, but they'd only just gotten together, and Alvin knew Roman had little experience. He wouldn't demand anything Roman wasn't ready to give.

He might not be perfect, but he was perfect for Roman. Roman was glad Alvin hadn't turned out to be the enemy, and he hoped everyone else—especially the council—would eventually realize that.

Roman yelped when Alvin rolled them so Roman was on his back. His instinct was to curl both of his legs around Alvin's, but he quickly stopped on the side where Alvin's wounded calf was. Alvin noticed and grabbed Roman's thigh, pulling it up until Roman could wrap his leg around his waist.

"Good?" Alvin asked.

Roman nodded. He felt unable to speak, and he was pretty sure that if he tried, only rubbish would come out. He was overwhelmed, but he loved it.

Alvin was in his arms, and his weight was heavy on top of Roman. Roman wouldn't have it any other way. If Alvin had been anyone else, he would have felt wary of the position, but not with him. He felt safe with Alvin and thought nothing of wrapping himself around his boyfriend and clinging to him like he was an octopus.

Alvin felt perfect on top of Roman. They kissed again, the heat between them rising as they both started to move. Roman had no idea what he was doing, but after trying to find a rhythm and failing, he paused and focused on Alvin.

Alvin was thrusting against Roman, and it was fairly easy to do the same once Roman stopped for a moment. With one of his legs wrapped around Alvin's and the other around Alvin's waist, Roman held on for dear life as their cocks slid together, trapped between their stomachs. He could never have imagined how perfect this would feel, but it did. He hadn't waited for his first sexual experience because he'd wanted to, but rather because he'd been forced to, but he was glad that Alvin was his first.

And hopefully, his only.

The way their bodies moved together made Roman want to scream. He didn't want to make a fool of himself, so he kissed Alvin. Alvin grunted and thrust harder. The friction between them was exquisite. Roman needed more, but at the same time, he felt like if he got more, he'd explode.

Alvin surrounded him completely, and Roman was happy to let him do whatever he wanted. Alvin continued moving and kissing Roman, seemingly able to read Roman's body and expression. He knew right away when Roman was about to come, and he moved harder, putting even more pressure on Roman's cock. Roman cried out and tried to hide his face with his forearm, but Alvin would have none of that. He caught Roman's hand and linked their fingers together on the mattress, hesitating for a second before leaning down and kissing Roman again.

That second during which they stared each other in the eyes was enough for Roman to come. He'd seen how much Alvin cared about him in Alvin's eyes, and knowing that he was loved pushed him over the edge.

He cried out and clung to Alvin as his world exploded. It only felt that way for a few moments because seconds later, it was rearranging itself, and Roman knew he wouldn't be able to live without Alvin anymore. Alvin was in his heart, and if he was kicked out of the forest, Roman would find a way to go with him.

It wouldn't be easy, but it would be worth it, and that was all Roman cared about. He'd finally found a place where he knew he belonged. He was in Alvin's heart as much as Alvin was in his, and both of them would fight to keep things that way.

No matter what that fight entailed.

Chapter Twelve

R oman was already smiling when he woke up and didn't think that would change anytime soon. How could it, when he'd never felt so happy in his life?

He'd had a few relationships before, but they hadn't been anything like this one. For one, he'd had to hide because Silas would never have allowed him to have a male lover. His head had probably exploded when he'd found out that Jasper had moved his human boyfriend in. Knowing how annoyed and angry he'd no doubt been made Roman giddy, but the feeling was nothing next to how he felt when he thought of Alvin.

Last night had been wonderful. Roman had known it would be because how could it not have been? Alvin was sweet, and even though he was quiet a lot of the time, it didn't make him any less passionate. He'd shown Roman how much he wanted him last night, and Roman wondered if they could have a repeat this morning.

He reached for his phone as he tried not to move too much so he wouldn't wake up Alvin. His boyfriend was plastered against his back, holding his waist as if he was afraid Roman would crawl out of bed during the night. Maybe that was how Alvin unconsciously felt. He might be an official surfeit member now, but Roman knew him. He had no doubt Alvin was still afraid something would happen that would force him to leave, and to be honest, Roman had similar fears.

No matter how much faith he had in Jasper, the council would have the final word when it came to Alvin. If they decided to kick him out, it would create trouble Jasper might not be ready to deal with. Luckily, they had allies, but without talking to them, it was hard to have faith in them.

Roman's movement to grab his phone must have jolted Alvin because Roman felt him move. Alvin's lips pressed against the back of Roman's neck, and Roman wiggled closer to his boyfriend, smiling like an idiot at the thought.

He had a boyfriend. He'd gone and fallen in love with a wounded human, and now, here they were.

"Good morning," Alvin said.

His voice was rough and sleepy, making Roman want to stay in bed the entire day.

He checked his phone. It was late, but thankfully, no one had called. That meant no one in the surfeit was in need of a healer, and he hoped that would continue for the rest of the day.

"Good morning," Roman said, dropping his phone onto the mattress.

He started to turn to face Alvin, but a loud knock on his front door stopped him. He glared, briefly wondered if he could ignore it, then decided he couldn't.

"Sorry about that," he said with a grimace.

Alvin kissed his forehead. "Don't worry. You're the surfeit healer, and I already know people might need you at any time of the day or night. I don't expect you to stop doing your job just because we're together."

Roman quickly kissed him, but another knock pushed him to get out of bed. He quickly got dressed, wondering what had happened. He worried about some of the older members of the surfeit, even though with Silas being only a memory, their lives were much better.

Roman didn't hesitate to open the door when he reached it, but he immediately regretted it. "What are you doing here?" he asked Foley.

The bat alpha tried to push past Roman, but Roman stood

his ground. He might be smaller, but this was his home, and he suspected Foley hadn't called Jasper this time, either. Once again, he'd come into skunk territory without talking to the alpha, and it made Roman angry. Knowing that Foley was here for Alvin didn't help things.

"We're here for the human," Foley snapped. "You protected him once, but that's over."

"What are you talking about?"

"There was another shooting," Lindsay said.

She was here today, too, along with the raccoon alpha. Roman wasn't surprised to see them with Foley, but he wished they would leave Alvin alone. "And you think he shot whoever the target was?"

"It has to be him," Foley insisted. "He's the only one who would do something like that."

Roman snorted. "He's not. Off the top of my head, I can think of at least two people who would do something like that, and so can you. I won't let you hurt Alvin just because you think he shot at someone."

"It's worse this time," Lindsay said. "Someone died."

Roman's stomach dropped. He'd expected someone to die eventually, but to hear it had happened was still a hit. He wanted to ask who had died, but his main focus had to be Alvin. Hopefully, he'd heard what was happening and would stay inside, but Roman wouldn't put it past him to try to hand himself over so that Foley wouldn't create trouble for Jasper and the surfeit.

Roman straightened his back and squared his shoulders. "I'm sorry to hear that, but it still doesn't explain what you're doing here. Alvin had nothing to do with any of the shootings, including this one."

"You can't be sure of that," Foley said. "He could have snuck out, and you wouldn't have noticed."

"I would *definitely* have noticed. He hasn't left the house since last night."

"Maybe he snuck past you," Russo said. "He snuck into the forest, and no one noticed him."

The man didn't talk much, but the few times he did open his mouth, it was to say something stupid.

"The circumstances are entirely different," Roman pointed out. "No one was hanging around the hole in the fence, so no one could see him sneak in. I was with him the entire night, wrapped around him. I would have noticed if he'd left my bed."

Foley looked like he was about to say something Roman didn't want to hear, so Roman glared at him. Unfortunately, it wasn't enough to get Foley to leave.

"We want the human, and you're going to hand him over," Foley said with a growl. "You might be a healer, but I'm an alpha. All three of us are."

"You might be an alpha, but you're also a dickhead. All three of you are, but I expected better from Lindsay. I'm not handing anyone over, and I'm not letting you into my home. You need to leave before Jasper arrives and kicks your ass. He wasn't happy the first time you did this, but he's going to be *pissed* this time."

Roman didn't expect the three to leave, but if they tried pushing into his home, he'd defend it and Alvin. No one was allowed inside, and no one was allowed to hurt his boyfriend.

He might be small in both of his forms, but that wouldn't stop him from kicking ass if he had to.

Alvin was terrified. He'd texted Jasper as soon as he'd realized what was happening on Roman's porch, but it didn't feel like enough. What was he supposed to do while he waited for Jasper to arrive? And even when Jasper did, would it be enough?

Just like last time, three alphas wanted Alvin, and only one alpha would fight to keep him here. Jasper wouldn't be able to do much if it came to that. He might even get hurt while trying to protect Alvin, and that wasn't something Alvin was willing to let happen.

He swallowed. He was standing by the living room entrance, just out of sight from the front door. He'd heard the entire conversation, so he knew that this time someone had died. He felt sorry for whoever had been hurt, but he'd had nothing to do with it.

He wasn't sure he'd be able to convince these people of that.

What would happen if he couldn't? His first instinct was to run, but he couldn't. He'd found something precious in surfeit territory and wouldn't let anyone or anything destroy it. He could tell Foley wanted to hurt him, but hopefully, if he handed himself over, the other two alphas would protect him long enough to hand him over to the council. The council wouldn't hurt Alvin, right? They just wanted him to get out of here.

But what if they believed Alvin had something to do with the shootings like Foley? If they did, they wouldn't let Alvin leave. They'd probably imprison him, and that was if he was lucky. He didn't know much about the laws and justice in the forest, but he knew it wasn't like the human justice system. The alphas and the council had the last word, and if there were enough votes for it, Alvin could be executed.

He shivered. He didn't want to die, but he wouldn't let anyone be hurt in his place. If this was what he had to do to protect Roman and Jasper, he'd do it.

"You're making it a habit of visiting my territory without calling first," Jasper said from somewhere behind the three alphas.

Alvin couldn't see him, but he was both relieved and

anxious at the thought of Jasper being there. He was the one with ultimate authority in this territory, but again, he was only one against three.

Foley turned, probably to face Jasper, and even though there was nothing he wanted less, Alvin moved to Roman's side. He touched Roman's back, and Roman looked alarmed when he realized he was behind him. He tried to push him away, but Alvin wouldn't hide.

He'd had nothing to do with this and had nothing to feel guilty for. There was no reason for him to hide.

"We just want the human," Lindsay said.

"And I want the three of you to stay out of my territory and leave my surfeit members alone, but I see that asking wasn't enough."

"Someone died this time, Jasper. You have to see this needs to be done."

Roman wouldn't let Alvin any closer than he already was. He was blocking Alvin's way to the porch, but Alvin could see around him well enough.

Jasper climbed the porch steps and came to stand in front of the door. "I'm sorry someone died, but Alvin had nothing to do with it. Beyond that, you were warned once that if you dared enter my territory without calling me first, I would go to the council. Since you just did it again, I have no choice but to do just that."

"The council will be on our side," Foley said.

"Will they? Because as far as I know, they're the only ones who can send people to the territories where they don't belong without prior authorization from the alpha. It's what their teams were created for, but you're not part of those teams. That means you're breaking the law."

"You're harboring a criminal," Foley snapped.

"Am I? Do you have proof?"

"I don't need proof. I know he was involved, no matter

what you and your healer say."

"I'm not letting you take Alvin. You don't have the authority to do so."

Alvin tried pushing past Roman again. "I'll go with them,"
he murmured.

Jasper heard him and quickly turned to glare at him.
"You're not going anywhere. You're innocent of what they're
accusing you of, and as your alpha, I'm ordering you to stand
back."

"You're not his alpha," Foley said. "He's just a human and
won't be alive for long anyway."

Alvin hadn't thought it possible, but Jasper's expression
hardened even more. He looked utterly disgusted by Foley —
a sentiment Alvin shared.

"No one will touch one hair on Alvin's head, including
you. Beyond that, I formally asked him to become a surfeit
member, and he agreed. That makes me his alpha and him my
responsibility. Since I knew you wouldn't understand that, I
contacted Olga back at the council. She'll bring this up at the
council meeting she called for."

Foley took a step forward. Alvin's heart jumped into his
throat, but Jasper didn't seem fazed. He barely even moved.

"It's our right to deal with any threat in the forest," Foley
growled.

"Then maybe you should focus on finding the shooter and
dealing with *them*. I have nothing else to say to you, and neither does Alvin. If you persist, I'll have to call my allies, and
while you might have time to create trouble before they arrive, both of us know you don't want to deal with the force of
the badgers and the bears. They would destroy your people,
and you'd lose all your power."

For a moment, Alvin was sure Foley was going to attack
anyway. He held his breath, ready to go with the bat alpha if
that was what needed to be done to save Jasper and Roman.

Thankfully, Foley wasn't as stupid as Alvin had thought he was. He took a step back, then another, and while he still looked ready to kill, he didn't touch Jasper.

"You'll pay for this," he said.

"I have no doubt you'll try to make me pay for it, but we both know I'm right. There's nothing you can do about it, Foley, and you need to understand that. You also need to understand that the next time you enter my territory without asking for permission, I won't hesitate to punish you as I see fit."

Foley jerked forward, but Russo grabbed his arm and pulled him back. Foley resisted, which wasn't a surprise. Alvin was relieved when Lindsay and Russo managed to drag him away and back to the car in which they'd arrived.

Alvin had a strong sense of déjà vu as he, Jasper, and Roman watched the car leave.

"This will happen again," Jasper said.

Alvin agreed. "That's why I should have gone with them. It would have given them what they wanted, and you and the surfeit would be safe."

Jasper shook his head. "You're not going anywhere. You're one of my people, and I wouldn't hand any of them over to those three. I'd even fight the council if they tried to take you."

"I don't want you or the surfeit to be in trouble," Alvin insisted.

Jasper squeezed his shoulder. "I already knew what would happen when I asked you to become a surfeit member. I expected the threats and the problems, and I don't want you to worry too much about that. I have allies, and I'm sure the surfeit will be fine. I don't regret taking you in or fighting for you. You deserve someone who will protect you, and I'll be that person."

"But this will happen again," Roman murmured. "We need to do something. I'm afraid that there will be more of them next time or that Foley will attack."

Jasper's expression was grim. "I agree. Alvin, I think you should leave the house for a bit and hide. There are plenty of places in our territory where you'd be safe, and no one will know to find you there. I know I'm asking a lot because you've just found your home with Roman, but it would be safer for both of you to be separated for a while. I need enough time to deal with the way these three entered our territory without calling me first. Once I'm sure the council has talked to them and explained the consequences if they try this again, you can come back."

Alvin didn't want to leave Roman, but he wasn't sure he had a choice. He'd do anything to protect Roman and the surfeit, and right now, the only thing he could do was leave them.

So he would.

CHAPTER THIRTEEN

The house was tiny, but that wasn't Alvin's main problem with it. No, Alvin's problem with the place was that Roman wasn't there.

He glared at the space around him. It was nice enough, and Jasper had promised that Alvin wouldn't have to stay very long. Alvin felt like a child who'd had his favorite toy taken away. It made him uncomfortable and angry at himself. Mostly, he was angry at the council and the alphas who'd hounded him.

Was it too much to ask to be left alone? These people knew he had nothing to do with the shootings, but they were looking for someone who wouldn't stand up to them and who wouldn't have support. They'd chosen him because he was human and had snuck into the forest, and they hadn't expected him to have people on his side.

He hadn't expected it either. As he leaned back on the small couch, he thought about his state of mind when he'd found the hole in the fence.

He'd been planning to get into the forest by any means necessary, and when he'd found a small hole in the fence, he'd known that was it. He needed just enough space to sneak through, and widening the hole had been fairly easy. He'd been terrified that someone would find him, but the forest was vast, and even with so many shifters living there, a lot of it was empty space.

That was how Alvin had managed to be left alone for so long. He'd lived in areas of the forest where no one else went.

He'd had to be careful because the people who lived close by shifted often and went for runs, but he'd managed.

Until he hadn't anymore.

He'd never have to live alone in the forest again. Jasper had promised that now that Alvin was a surfeit member, it was his right to live with the skunks and settle down here, and Alvin had every intention of doing just that. Unfortunately for him, it wouldn't be as easy as he wished. The council and the alphas were making it harder, but it wouldn't last forever.

Or at least, Alvin hoped it wouldn't.

He'd been starving but content when he'd been on his own in the forest, but he didn't feel that way anymore. Now, he had something to lose, or rather, someone.

He didn't want to be away from Roman, and Roman didn't want to be away from him. They'd agreed to it because they didn't have a choice, but Alvin hoped it wouldn't be for long. Jasper was working hard to make the council see that they should be lenient with Alvin, talking to his allies and explaining everything, and Alvin prayed he'd succeed.

But if Jasper failed, Alvin was ready to live in this tiny cabin in the woods for the rest of his life. He could still see Roman as often as possible, and he'd be safe here. It would become lonely after a while, but Alvin was used to loneliness and didn't mind it.

A scratch at the door made him jump up from the couch. He rushed to open it, pausing only a few seconds to peek out the window. He couldn't see anyone, but he opened the door anyway because he knew who it was.

A small skunk was waiting in front of the door. It scurried inside as soon as there was enough space for it to come through, and Alvin watched the bundle of black and white fur as it rushed past him.

He grinned and closed the door before leaning against it. Roman didn't stay in his skunk form for long. He shifted as soon as the door was closed and threw himself into Alvin's arms. Alvin caught him, holding him close and burying his face into his hair.

"I'm okay," he promised.

"I know. I wasn't worried you wouldn't be okay. I just missed you."

Alvin smiled. "I miss you, too."

He wouldn't have believed it if anyone had told him he'd be in this position a few months ago. His beginning in the forest had been harsh, and he'd almost died, but he'd gained so much that he couldn't regret it. He didn't even care that he'd always bear the scars of the coyote attack on his calf. He could have done without them, but Roman didn't mind them, and while Alvin knew he was weaker than before and might always walk with a limp, he'd learn to deal with it. It didn't take away from the way his life had changed and how he'd gotten everything he'd ever dreamed of.

"You should get dressed," Alvin said as he rubbed Roman's back. "You're going to get cold."

Roman leaned away. "Maybe *you* could make sure I don't get cold."

Alvin's body went hot at the suggestion. Now that he and Roman were together, it felt like they didn't spend enough time as a couple. It was probably because they'd been separated, and once again, Alvin told himself it wouldn't last forever. Even if he had to stay here for a month, Roman would be waiting for him when he left, and that was all that mattered.

Alvin grinned and grabbed Roman. He hauled him into his arms, ignoring the squeak coming from his boyfriend, and moved toward the bed. This was the only thing he liked about the cabin—it was only one room, which meant the bed was always close by.

Like every time they saw each other after spending time

separated, Roman and Alvin moved desperately. Alvin's clothes didn't stay on for long, and once they were gone, their need took over. Alvin yearned to feel Roman on his skin, maybe even inside of him, but neither of them was willing to go slow. They rutted against each other, almost as if they felt they wouldn't get another chance to do this.

They would. Alvin wouldn't consider any other outcome.

Eventually, they flopped back onto the bed. Alvin stared at the ceiling as he tried to catch his breath and wondered how he'd been so lucky. He didn't know, but he'd cherish Roman and everything Roman was willing to give him for the rest of his life.

Roman snuggled close. "Jasper told me he'd be visiting you in a few hours."

"That means we'll have to get dressed."

"We will, but not right now."

Alvin wanted to make the most out of the time he and Roman had together, and he felt that was better done in bed. After making love, they talked briefly about Roman's patients and how the rest of his life was going without Alvin. Alvin didn't have a lot to say since he was stuck here on his own, and it was a delight to hear Roman talk about the people he worked with. Alvin loved the time they spent alone together but also enjoyed having Jasper visiting him, so he quickly opened the door when the alpha finally got there.

Jasper arched a brow. "Did you even check who it was?"

"Of course," Alvin lied. "Besides, Roman told me you were coming."

Jasper came in. "I wish I had good news for you."

And there went Alvin's happiness. "You don't?"

"Unfortunately, no. The council is still angry that I made you a surfeit member, but I know that if I hadn't, they would have kicked you out. They can't anymore, but it doesn't mean they will accept it easily. They're looking for a way out."

"Will they find one?"

Jasper sighed. "Possibly. I talked with a few people, and while they're wary about your presence here, they're willing to give you a chance. I have a meeting with Thomas, the badger alpha, and several other alphas he thinks we can convince right after this. He's firmly on our side, and I hope that between his council member and mine, we can have the council let this go. They have better things to focus on, and they know it."

"I want to come with you to see Thomas," Roman said.

"I don't think it's necessary," Jasper said gently. "He doesn't need to talk to you in order to decide that this is the best thing for everyone."

"Maybe not, but I want this to be over. If I have to talk to every single alpha to make that happen, I will, and since you said several of them would be there, I can do so more easily."

Alvin was overwhelmed by the support. Even if Jasper and Roman were the only two people on his side, he'd never had this before. Knowing that there were more people out there, like Dean and possibly the badger alpha, who were willing to help, made Alvin want to cry.

He wasn't alone anymore.

Roman was done with all of this. He'd had enough of having to sneak around, of being alone in his bed, and of Alvin being hidden like a shameful secret.

Alvin might be human, but he was a surfeit member. He'd had nothing to do with the shootings, which meant the council had no right to come after him for that. Roman might not have been present at the meetings Jasper had with them, but he knew what had happened. Jasper had told him and Alvin. He wasn't keeping any secrets, which was a relief because that meant Roman knew where they stood.

The council had tried to put the shootings on Alvin's shoulders, possibly pushed by Alpha Foley and his friends. Roman hoped Lindsay had nothing to do with that, but even if she did, it wasn't like they were friends. He'd hoped she would be different from her father as an alpha, and he still did, but she was on the wrong side for now.

No matter how hard they'd tried, the council couldn't pin anything on Alvin. They might have been able to if the only shootings had happened around the time he snuck into the forest, but that wasn't the case. There had been more, and someone had died during the last one. It couldn't have been Alvin because he'd still been healing from the devastating wound on his calf in Roman's house. Arlene had talked to the council along with Roman, and she'd assured the council members that Alvin wouldn't have been able to walk anywhere, let alone escape a group of angry shifters who wanted revenge.

With that out of the way, there wasn't really a reason for the council to keep doing this, but they were dragging things out, and Roman had no doubt they were doing it to make Jasper pay. He'd made things complicated for them when he'd welcomed Alvin into the surfeit, and they wanted him to be aware of that.

Jasper *was* aware of it, and he wasn't the only one.

Roman didn't know who in the council was holding back the decision, but he was sure it wasn't Olga, and he doubted it was the council members for the bears and the badgers. It probably wasn't the coyote, either. Roman knew how close Jasper was to those three alphas, and even more so, he knew the alphas themselves. Josiah had only just recently taken his father's place, but the few times Roman had talked to him, he'd seemed like a good guy. His partner was human, so he could understand Alvin's position better than most. Luther had reassured Jasper that the human government didn't know about Alvin and wouldn't find out through his team, which had been a relief.

As for the badgers and the bears, both Thomas and Morris were helping Jasper find his footing in his new alpha role. They were firmly on his side, meaning they wouldn't order their council members to complicate things.

That left all the others.

Roman didn't know those council members personally, so it would be pointless to talk to them, but he could talk to Thomas and see if he had any idea of how they could solve this problem. It might be enough to finally get it over with, but Roman didn't have a lot of hope.

Going to the meeting with Jasper meant that Roman couldn't spend as much time with Alvin as he'd hoped, but he told himself that this would be over soon, and when it was, they'd spend the rest of their lives together. It was what carried him through saying goodbye to Alvin and heading to Jasper's house to grab his truck.

"I'm really sorry you have to go through all of this," Jasper said once they were on the road.

He'd been silent since he and Roman had left the cabin where Alvin lived.

"It's not your fault, so you don't need to apologize. Do you know who else will be at the meeting?"

"Thomas said he was talking to other alphas, and I hope he convinced as many of them as possible so you can talk to them. You're the one who knows Alvin the best, so hopefully, they'll listen to you. I know Thomas is close to some of these alphas. While I understand why they're wary, I'm hoping that between what you'll say and Thomas's support, they'll ask their council members to make the right decision."

"Some of them might think that the right decision is to kick Alvin out," Roman pointed out.

"Possibly, but I don't see what it would change for them.

Alvin is a surfeit member. That means that even once he's free to leave the cabin where he's staying right now, he'll stay in our territory. His life will be here, and he won't be a danger to any of the other alphas or anyone else. Hell, he's not a danger now, but I understand why they might think he is."

"We need to convince them that he had nothing to do with the shootings."

"I'm not sure how to do that beyond explaining what happened to him again and insisting that he couldn't walk, let alone run around the forest with a gun."

Roman squared his shoulders. He was ready to go into excruciating detail if it meant the council listened to him. He'd noticed how Olga and Karen had reacted when they'd seen the wound on Alvin's calf. They'd been able to tell how bad it was, which meant they had to know he hadn't been going around shooting at people. They were only two council members, and Ronald was actively working against Alvin, but he didn't have that much support.

Roman was nervous the entire way to the meeting. There were more cars parked in front of Thomas's house than he'd expected, so he took a deep breath before following Jasper in.

Things in Thomas's office were tense, but Thomas behaved as if he didn't notice it. He welcomed Jasper and Roman, not looking surprised to see Roman there even though he hadn't known he was coming.

"What's he doing here?" one of the alphas asked.

Roman narrowed his eyes at him. "Alpha Wiley," he said, lightly inclining his head. "It's good to see you're fully healed."

The bobcat alpha had been shot a while ago, but he hadn't been killed. One of his sons had taken over the alpha position while he was still healing, but from what Roman knew, that was over. Alpha Wiley was back in charge, which explained his presence here.

"Roman is close to Alvin and wanted to talk to you about him," Jasper explained.

"I wanted to tell you that what your council members are doing isn't fair." Roman looked around the office. He knew these people, although he hadn't talked to all of them. They probably didn't trust him, but he didn't care.

"I'm the skunk healer. I took Janice's place after Silas killed her. I might only be a healer, but I've lived through a lot when Silas was the alpha. I know dangerous people when I see them, and Alvin isn't dangerous. He's a human with shifters in his family tree, just like Dean and his family. They were allowed to move in with the foxes, so why shouldn't Alvin be allowed to move into the forest? Jasper has already made him a surfeit member, and he won't change his mind. None of you will have to deal with Alvin if he's allowed to stay, so you don't have to worry about that. You don't have to worry about anything. You just have to do the right thing."

"How can we be sure he wasn't behind the shootings?" Alpha Wiley asked.

"Can we agree that the same person shot both you and everyone else involved?" Roman asked.

Alpha Wiley nodded. "It would be too much of a coincidence to have two different people trying to kill alphas."

"Alvin was wounded recently. I've been taking care of him, and he hasn't been able to move. He can now, but he has a limp, and he always will. That means someone would have caught him if he'd been going around the forest shooting at people."

The alphas had to have already known that, but hopefully, hearing it from Roman would make them believe it. Roman had said his piece, and since the only thing left for him to do was drop to his knees and beg, he snapped his mouth shut and held back.

He couldn't force anyone to change their mind. He'd been

honest with them. Hopefully, they'd make the right choice.

As soon as they were done with this meeting, Roman would be going back to Alvin, and hopefully, he'd never have to leave him again.

Alvin was in the shower when he heard a car stop in front of the cabin. Roman had promised he'd return after the meeting, so Alvin rushed out of the shower, barely drying up, and threw on the first t-shirt and jeans he could find before shoving his feet into his shoes. Roman still wasn't in the cabin when Alvin finished, so Alvin decided to go outside and investigate.

He opened the door and glanced out. Jasper's car was gone, which wasn't a surprise, but Roman was nowhere to be seen, which was. Where was he?

"Step away from the front door," a voice said from Alvin's left.

Alvin froze. He recognized that voice and had a name to go with it now.

Harvey had found him.

He swallowed and stepped away from the door, glad he'd put on shoes. He was cold because he was still damp, but he didn't care. Had the car not belonged to Jasper? Alvin hoped it hadn't because that would mean that Roman wasn't here yet.

His stomach dropped when he saw that his boyfriend had arrived. He'd probably rushed out of Jasper's truck toward the front door, but it looked like Harvey had intercepted him before he could reach it. Alvin didn't understand how Jasper hadn't seen him, but that didn't matter now.

Harvey had been hiding along the side of the cabin. He had Roman pressed against him, back against his chest, and he was holding a gun to Roman's head. With his free arm, he guided Roman forward, never letting go as if he knew Alvin would react if he did.

Alvin wanted to, but he was terrified. He didn't want that gun to go off. It would be too easy for Roman to be hurt, and Alvin couldn't handle that.

"Harvey," he said.

"You know my name."

"Roman and Jasper told me who you are. What do you want?" Alvin had no idea why this man would want anything from him, which had to mean he was here for Roman. Why? Was someone in his little group of traitors hurt?

"Can you imagine my surprise when I learned that Jasper welcomed you into the surfeit? This place was supposed to be mine. I was supposed to be the alpha until Silas returned, but Jasper ruined everything."

"You would have been awful alpha," Roman grumbled.

Alvin wanted to tell him it probably wasn't the best idea to offend the guy holding a gun to his temple, but he didn't dare. Besides, Harvey behaved as if he hadn't heard Roman. His attention was fully on Alvin, and Alvin wanted things to stay that way.

"But that's fine," Harvey continued. "I found a way to get rid of you and get Silas out of jail at the same time, so in the end, you'll be useful."

"So it's me you want?" Alvin asked.

"Why would I want a healer?" Harvey asked. "He's only useful to me because he means you'll follow me without doing anything stupid."

"I will," Alvin assured him. "But only if you let him go."

"Don't do this," Roman said. "He's going to kill you."

Alvin held his boyfriend's gaze. "Probably, but that's all right. As long as you're safe, I don't care what happens to me."

Harvey gave Roman a good shake. "Shut it. He already

said he's coming with me."

Roman tried to get away, but Harvey didn't let go of his shoulder. From the way Roman grimaced, Alvin could tell Harvey's hold on him was hard and painful. He wanted to do something, but Harvey still held a gun to Roman's head.

"Just stay calm," Alvin told Roman.

"Yes, Roman, just stay calm," Harvey mocked. "I don't need you anymore. I thought this was going to be harder."

Roman pulled on Harvey's hold again. "Let both of us go. Jasper's going to kill you when he finds you."

"He won't find me."

Alvin knew what Harvey was going to do before he did it. He cried out and jerked forward, but the sound of the gunshot reached him before he could take a step forward.

Roman's body dropped to the ground. Alvin rushed forward. This couldn't be happening.

He knelt by Roman's side. There was blood on Roman's temple, and Alvin felt like he couldn't breathe. He leaned closer, holding his breath as he tried to find out if Roman was alive, but Harvey grabbed his shoulder and pulled him back.

"There's no need to cry over his body. He's gone, and you're coming with me."

Alvin ignored Harvey and pushed forward. He managed to grab Roman and haul him into his arms. His breath hitched when he realized Roman was still breathing. From what Alvin could hear, his heartbeat was steady, strong, and very much there.

Roman was alive.

Harvey pulled Alvin back again, and this time, Alvin went with it. Roman was alive, even though he was unconscious. Alvin needed to make sure that Harvey didn't realize that because if he did, he'd shoot Roman again, and this time, he'd make sure Roman died.

Alvin sucked in a breath. "You killed him."

The tears prickling his eyes were real. Even though Roman was alive, he was bleeding and unconscious, and Alvin couldn't stay with him to ensure he was all right. That meant that Roman would wake up alone in the forest—if he woke up at all.

Alvin needed to have faith. Roman was breathing, so he'd be all right. He had to be.

"I didn't need him anymore," Harvey said, his tone nonchalant as if he was talking about spoiled milk. "Now get up and come with me. I have plans for you."

Alvin obeyed. He stumbled to his feet and quickly moved back from Roman, wanting Harvey to be as far away from him as possible. Harvey seemed delighted that Alvin was following his orders and pushed him toward the side of the cabin. Alvin walked on, even though he felt like he'd left his heart behind.

The only thing he could do was pray that Roman would be all right and wake up soon. Alvin didn't even care if Roman managed to raise the alarm and have someone come for him. He'd willingly die if it meant Roman was all right.

He just hoped he wouldn't have to go that far.

Alvin had enough of people ruining his life and destroying the happiness he'd found in the forest. He wanted to scream at Harvey that it wasn't fair, but he kept his mouth shut and followed Harvey's orders. Even if Roman didn't send anyone after Alvin, Alvin would find a way out of this. He wasn't giving up, dammit.

The life he and Roman were building would be waiting for him once all of this was over, and he had every intention of getting back to it. If he could escape Harvey, he could come back and check on Roman. He'd take care of his boyfriend for once instead of Roman taking care of him.

But for now, caring for Roman meant going with Harvey, and the thought was petrifying. Alvin had no way of knowing what would happen to him or what Harvey was planning. He wasn't sure he wanted to find out, but he had to if he wanted a chance to make it out.

That was all he needed. A chance to return to his life. A chance to have his happiness and to be allowed to live in the forest permanently.

A chance to make everyone in the forest see that he wasn't the enemy.

Harvey was.

CHAPTER FOURTEEN

Alvin hadn't been surprised when Harvey had dragged him to a car parked nearby. It would have made sense for him to drive if he'd been planning to take Alvin with him. He knew Alvin was human and wouldn't be able to shift, but even if Alvin had been a shifter, Harvey probably wouldn't have wanted him to shift. It would have been much harder to control him if Alvin had become an opossum.

Alvin wasn't a shifter. He was human, and he was stuck with Harvey.

The doors were locked, and Harvey was driving. He'd tied Alvin's hands together, but even if Alvin managed to get free, he wouldn't be going anywhere. Harvey was too close, and he was keeping an eye on him. He wouldn't allow Alvin to do anything that might ruin his plans, whatever they were.

Alvin was terrified, but he was also curious. He'd heard a lot about Harvey from Jasper and Roman, so he knew that Harvey had been a loyal beta to Jasper's father. Silas was in jail, but Alvin remembered the conversation he'd heard in the forest right before he'd been wounded.

Harvey was planning to get Silas out of jail.

Alvin didn't understand what his role was in all of this. Why did Harvey need him? He was human, and apart from Roman, Jasper, and a few other people, no one would come for him. The other alphas and the council would probably be relieved if something happened to Alvin. It would mean they didn't have to deal with the problems he was causing by being in the forest.

But whatever Harvey had in mind for Alvin, it couldn't be good. It might even end in Alvin's death, so he decided he might as well ask questions.

"Where are you taking me?" he asked.

Harvey kept his focus on the road. He stayed silent, but Alvin didn't expect to get an answer. He'd already decided he wouldn't push because he wanted to stay alive if he could, but Harvey finally opened his mouth.

"We're going to free my alpha."

Just like Alvin had expected. He didn't know how Harvey planned to do that, but it seemed to involve him. "What do I have to do with all of this? Why did you take me?"

"Because I need someone to take the blame for freeing Silas, and who better than a human who shouldn't be in the forest? That'll show the council that no human should be allowed in. They wanted to lock us up, so now they don't have a choice in who we want in our forest. Wait until Silas is back. He'll set everyone on the right path."

Probably by killing the people he disliked and using violence and threats on the others. The thought made Alvin shiver, even though he probably wouldn't be alive to see all of this.

Harvey was smarter than Alvin had expected. Most of the people who knew about his presence in the forest didn't trust him, so they wouldn't be surprised to find out he had something to do with Silas's escape. If Alvin made it out of this, they might not even want to listen to what he had to say about it. Even if they did listen to him, there was no way they'd believe he had nothing to do with this. Harvey would probably drag Alvin right in the middle of things, which meant that someone would see him there and come to the conclusion that Alvin had snuck into the forest to do this.

Would Roman believe it? Would Jasper?

Alvin prayed they wouldn't. Roman had been there when

Harvey had attacked, so he knew Alvin hadn't gone along willingly. Unfortunately, there was no way to know if he would wake up.

Alvin sucked in a breath. He wanted to cry, scream, curl into a tight ball, and ignore the rest of the world, but he couldn't. Roman was alive, and there was a good chance he'd fully heal from what Harvey had done to him. When he did, Alvin wanted to be by his side. That meant he couldn't let fear and pain take over. He'd have to fight, but that was what he'd been doing since he was a kid. He could do it this time, too. Once it was over, he'd have a happy and easy life, and *that* was what he needed to focus on.

Alvin wasn't sure how long they drove, but he knew where they were headed, so he wasn't surprised when Harvey stopped at a distance from a big building. They stayed in the car, and while Alvin had more questions, he decided he didn't need to ask them. Even if Harvey told him what he was planning, Alvin doubted it would help him. He'd have to see what happened in the moment and make his decisions on the fly.

He didn't have to wait long before things started moving. Two cars parked next to Harvey's, and after glaring at him, Harvey went to talk to the men who came out of them. One had to be the coyote who'd bitten Alvin, and Alvin had to work hard not to throw up. He kind of wanted to because it would annoy Harvey, but he couldn't be sure these guys wouldn't hurt him.

Including Harvey, there were five men. Alvin wondered if there were more waiting somewhere to step in if Harvey needed them. He seemed to be in charge, which wasn't a surprise since Silas was his alpha.

What also wasn't a surprise was to see that all of them had masks they put on. The only one who wouldn't be wearing one was Alvin, which he thought was a bit stupid but might just work. Some people would wonder why he hadn't covered his face, but others would be more than happy to point a finger at him and accuse him of letting Silas out. They wouldn't care that he was here because he'd been forced to.

He swallowed when Harvey turned toward the car and came closer. This was it. Whatever happened next, Alvin had to be careful and ready to act. If he got even one chance to escape, he had to take it.

"Get out," Harvey ordered when he opened the door.

Alvin obeyed. The only thing that would happen if he didn't was that Harvey would drag him out of the car, and it wouldn't help Alvin. He could already tell that he was going with Harvey one way or another, and if he wanted to escape, he had to be in good enough shape to run when the opportunity presented itself. That meant not letting Harvey hurt him.

"You really think they're going to believe this?" one of the men asked when Alvin and Harvey reached the group.

"Why shouldn't they?" Harvey asked. "They already suspect him to be behind the shootings. They'll be happy to accuse him of this, too, and put him behind bars."

The other man's lips curled in disgust. "We should kill him."

Harvey laughed. "I'm not saying I disagree, but he'll be more useful to us alive."

And if he wasn't, they wouldn't hesitate to kill him. Alvin heard the words that weren't said, and they made him want to run. Instead, he allowed Harvey to push him toward the building in the distance.

They had to walk through the forest for a bit, but it wasn't long before they reached the back of the building. There was a fence running all around it, with barbed wire on top.

They'd reached the jail.

To Alvin's surprise, Harvey and his friends didn't try to sneak in. Instead, they went right to a gate, and Harvey made a short phone call. Seconds later, the gate clicked open, and Harvey pushed Alvin inside.

They followed the path down to a back door, which opened, too. A man was waiting for them on the other side, and since he was wearing a guard's uniform, Alvin knew what had happened.

Harvey had an ally inside the jail.

Knowing that, it would be easy for Harvey to get Silas out. Was there anything Alvin could do to make sure that didn't happen? He didn't think so. Even if he started screaming for help, would anyone but the men holding him hostage hear him? And if anyone did, would they believe him? He was with these people, and it probably looked like he was part of their group to an outsider.

When Harvey pushed Alvin forward, Alvin obeyed the silent order and started walking. He kept glancing around, but no matter how hard he looked, he couldn't see anything or anyone who might help. They walked along hallways, passing locked doors that held silent prisoners. Where were all the guards? Two of the men who'd met Harvey outside the jail left their group and headed in another direction.

The place wasn't huge, so it wasn't long before they stopped in front of one of the doors. Alvin swallowed, suddenly even more nervous.

"I'll let him out, but I have to go," the guard said. "I need to be in my place when the alarm goes off."

"Do it," Harvey ordered.

The guard unlocked the door and quickly stepped back. He didn't wait to watch Silas leave his cell. He rushed down the hallway, quickly disappearing around the corner.

The door opened. Alvin couldn't look away from the man standing there. He looked like Jasper, but there was a hardness to him that told Alvin that this man was nothing like his friend. He wouldn't be in jail if he were.

"Finally," Silas drawled. He paused and arched a brow when he caught sight of Alvin. "What is this?"

Harvey stepped forward and shook Silas's hand. "Our red herring. This is the human the council is fighting over."

Silas looked amused. "They won't be fighting over him for much longer."

Alvin was sure that if Silas had his way, he'd die before the council could make any kind of decision about him, and even if he didn't, they'd believe he'd freed Silas and would never allow him to stay. They might not even allow him out of this jail.

He had to do something, but what?

Roman's head ached when he woke up. For a moment, that was all he could focus on. It felt like his brain was about to explode, and he didn't know how to deal with it.

He was a healer. He'd never been in so much pain, but he knew what to do. He'd helped countless people with *their* pain, and while it was a little more complicated, he could do so with himself, too.

He forced his eyes open. He already knew Alvin would be gone, but the fear that gripped him was enough to make him need to move. He tried to ignore the pain as he rolled to his knees and then got into a sitting position. Rising to his feet felt like too much right now, so sitting it would be.

Once he was stable, he reached up to touch his forehead. Harvey had shot him. He wasn't sure how he was alive, but he'd never forget what it had felt like. He'd thought for sure he would die, and he was stunned that he hadn't.

Roman's last thought had been that if he died, no one would be able to warn Jasper and the others of what was happening. That was what had pushed him to move sideways when he'd realized what Harvey was about to do and what had saved him. He'd be dead if he hadn't moved, and Alvin would be lost.

Roman wasn't dead, and he needed to move. He had no idea how long he'd been unconscious, but it had to have been long enough for Harvey to take Alvin wherever he needed him. Roman would never forgive himself if something happened to Alvin. It didn't matter that he'd been shot and that he was bleeding. Right now, he only cared about Harvey and Alvin and stopping whatever was about to happen.

He fumbled for his phone. It was in his jacket pocket, but even though it shouldn't be hard for him to get it, his hands made it complicated. They shook hard, and one was dirty with blood, but he ignored it as he finally grabbed his phone and dialed Jasper's number.

"Alvin?" the alpha asked when he answered. "Everything all right? I didn't expect to hear from you until tomorrow."

"Harvey was here when I arrived. He waited for you to drive away to grab me," Roman quickly said. "He wanted Alvin. He shot me, so I don't know where he took Alvin, but we both know what he was planning."

Jasper swore. "He went to break my father out."

"Yes. We need to go."

"I'm coming to pick you up. You say Harvey shot you?"

"I was lucky, but I'm going to need medical attention." Roman might as well be honest because Jasper would realize it as soon as he saw him. He just hoped it wouldn't be bad enough that Jasper would try to convince him to stay back. He was going after Alvin, and that was that.

"I'll grab the first aid kit, but if you need more, we'll have to contact Arlene."

"We can deal with that later. Please, Jasper. I can't leave Alvin with Harvey."

"We're not."

Jasper was true to his word. He reached Roman as quickly

as he could, considering the distance between the two houses, and when Roman climbed into the passenger seat of his car, he found a first aid kid waiting for him. Jasper sucked in a breath when he saw him, but Roman ignored him and opened the kit after putting on his seatbelt.

The last thing he needed was to end up in a car accident and hurt himself even worse.

"I know you'll say no, but you should see Arlene," Jasper tried as he drove away.

"As soon as I have Alvin back. I want her to check him, too."

Jasper nodded. "I've been on the phone since you called me. I warned Thomas of what was happening, so we'll be meeting him there."

That was good. They had allies, and it was time they stepped up and did the right thing. Thomas always had, but some of the other alphas had understandably kept out of the mess. If they didn't change that now, they would end up with Jasper's father in charge of the surfeit again, and no one wanted that.

There wasn't a lot of light in the truck, but Roman made do. He quickly cleaned the wound on his forehead, relieved when he realized he wouldn't need stitches. He'd been lucky. If he hadn't moved, the bullet would have killed him. As it was, it had burned a wound into his temple. He closed it with butterfly bandages, using the mirror in the sun visor to place them. Arlene might insist on doing something different when she saw him, but for now, this was fine. Roman didn't care about scars. He just wanted his boyfriend back.

Jasper's phone rang when they were almost there. Roman had never visited the council jail. He'd never needed to, and he hoped he would never have to return. But he knew where it was because he'd made a point of finding out after Silas had been imprisoned. He'd wanted to know where the old alpha was.

"We're almost there," Jasper said as he put the phone on speaker.

"Good. I have bad news," Thomas said.

Roman and Jasper briefly looked at each other.

"He escaped?" Jasper asked.

"He's certainly not in his cell anymore, but it's a bit of a mess here. The alarm was blaring when we arrived, and the guards were running around. I immediately checked Silas's cell and found it empty, but there's no way to know if he's still on the property."

"We'll be careful. What about Alvin?"

"I'm not sure. I haven't found him yet."

That wasn't what Roman had wanted to hear, but he wasn't surprised. Whatever Harvey had planned for Alvin, he would have put that plan into gear when they reached the jail. Roman prayed he hadn't hurt his boyfriend, but knowing both Harvey and Silas, he was alarmed.

It wasn't fair. He and Alvin had finally found happiness. It hadn't been easy, and Alvin might still lose it because of the council, but Roman was ready to fight for this. Alvin was, too, but how could he fight if he was hurt—or worse?

Roman felt like he was about to lose everything he'd ever dreamed of, and it made him want to scream. He was terrified of what he'd find at the jail, but at the same time, he couldn't avoid going there. He needed to know.

If something had happened to Alvin, Roman would take care of him. It was the least Alvin deserved, and Roman was ready to give him his everything, whether he was dead or alive.

Alvin hadn't known what to expect after Silas had been let out of his cell, but it wasn't to be dragged back to the exit.

They wanted him to take the blame for letting Silas out, so why were they taking him away? Maybe Harvey would kill Alvin and make everyone think a guard had caught him on his way out.

It didn't matter. The alarm was blaring, a sure sign that someone had noticed something was wrong, and Alvin and the others were almost at the exit. Alvin needed to do something before they reached it because otherwise, it would be too late.

He didn't like any of this. Harvey and Silas were talking, ignoring the alarm as if it wasn't loud enough to shake the walls. The other men kept looking at the two, and Alvin wondered if this was what they'd expected. He understood why Harvey had wanted to get Silas out since Silas had been his alpha, but what about the others? At least one of them was a coyote shifter, so why was he so interested in Silas?

It didn't matter. Alvin was curious, but right now, what mattered the most was to get out of there alive. With Harvey focused on Silas, he wasn't looking at Alvin, which meant Alvin had a chance to run. He'd have to be fast, and he'd have to choose the right moment, but he was ready.

He had to be because they were almost at the exit.

They turned the corner, and a guard appeared. He was pale but raised his gun and yelled at them to stop. They did, but probably not because they were afraid of the guard.

He wasn't surprised when Harvey launched forward to attack. He wanted to help the guard, but it was him or Alvin, and Alvin wasn't selfless. Everyone was focused on the fight, so Alvin took advantage of that.

With his good foot, he stomped on the toes of the guy holding his arm. The guy jerked back, and Alvin elbowed him in the stomach and turned, slamming his knee into the man's groin.

He'd never been so glad for the few self-defense classes

he'd taken.

The man went down, clutching his groin, but Alvin didn't stick around to find out how he was.

He heard people yell behind him, but he tried to focus on what was in front of him. He turned the corner, not knowing where he was going. He just knew he had to get away from Harvey and Silas.

"Stop!" someone yelled in front of him.

It was a guard. It wasn't the one who'd let Harvey and Alvin in, and Alvin prayed he'd be one of the good guys. This guard had a gun, too, so Alvin wasn't going anywhere.

He stopped running and raised his hands. "Please. I have nothing to do with what's happening. Harvey took me from my home and brought me here so I'd take the blame."

Another guard appeared. They both looked on edge, which was understandable. Alvin didn't expect them to believe him and didn't need them to. Even if they locked him up, at least he'd be alive and would have a chance to explain what had happened.

"Where did you take the prisoner?" the second guard asked.

"I wasn't the person who let him out."

"We saw you on the cameras," the first guard said as he reached Alvin and pushed him toward the wall.

Alvin pressed his front to the cold cement and allowed the guard to frisk him. He didn't have any weapons on him, so it didn't take long.

"I told you. I was brought here so people would think I was involved, but I had nothing to do with any of this. The old skunk beta did everything, along with his allies."

"Sure they did."

The guard sounded like he didn't believe Alvin. To be fair, Alvin wasn't sure he'd have believed himself considering the circumstances. The alarm was still blaring, and when the guard pushed Alvin toward the end of the hallway, he saw a body on the ground.

Alvin had no idea what had happened, but he didn't remember coming this way before, so it couldn't be Silas and Harvey. It certainly hadn't been him.

"I need to talk to someone," he begged.

"Our alpha will want to see you," one of the guards said.

Alvin swallowed. He didn't know what kind of shifter these guys were, so he had no clue who their alpha was. Hopefully, it would be an ally, but what if it wasn't? What if these two were bat shifters? Alpha Foley would be more than happy to lock Alvin up and throw away the key.

Alvin realized what had happened as they continued walking. Some of the cell doors were open, a sure sign that more prisoners had escaped. That would explain why not everyone who'd entered the jail with Harvey had followed him to Silas's cell. They'd either wanted to free some of their people or had created a distraction. Either way, it had worked, and Silas and Harvey were probably long gone.

Unfortunately, Alvin wasn't. He had to let the guards push him around until they reached a room that looked like it was used by jail personnel. There was a small fridge in the corner, a table and four chairs, and a microwave next to the coffee machine.

A man stood inside, talking on the phone, but he hung up when he saw Alvin.

"What's this?" he asked.

"Alpha Callahan," one of the guards said as he inclined his head. "We found this man running down the hallway."

"He's the man we saw on the CCTV."

"He is."

"I know I was on the cameras, but that's because Harvey forced me to come," Alvin said. "Please. I had nothing to do with this. I don't know Silas, but from what I heard about him, no one would have wanted him out of his cell. I certainly didn't."

"Yet you're on camera with Harvey and his accomplices, letting Silas out of his cell," Alpha Callahan said.

Alvin tried to remember which alpha he was, but he couldn't. He was panicking, and that was the last thing he needed. If he wanted to make it out of the situation, he had to keep calm.

It felt impossible to do.

"We'll deal with him once this mess is over," Alpha Callahan said. "Put him in the nearest cell."

"Please," Alvin begged. "You have to call Jasper. He's my alpha."

The words sounded odd in Alvin's voice, but they were true. Jasper *was* his alpha, and he'd be pissed when he found out about this.

Alpha Callahan's eyebrows rose on his forehead, but he didn't tell the guards to stop. He let them take Alvin out of the room and to the cell closest to it.

The guard pushed Alvin inside, and Alvin stumbled. He caught himself on one of the walls and turned, but there wasn't time for him to beg again. The door slammed shut behind the guard, and the sound of the lock was ominous.

Alvin swallowed. The situation was dire, but he had to look at it without panicking. He might be locked up, but that didn't mean he'd stay here forever. For now, Alpha Callahan didn't know if he could trust him, so it made sense to want Alvin locked up. Alvin was sure that once this mess was over and the jail was under control, someone would come, and he'd finally be able to talk to Jasper.

They wouldn't leave him here without talking to him. He had to believe that.

He had to believe that whatever happened next, he'd be allowed to go home to Roman.

Roman could hear the alarm blaring even before setting foot inside the jail. It hurt his ears, and between that and the wound, it felt like his headache would never end. He'd taken some painkillers from the first aid kit, but they weren't working yet.

He'd have to push through the pain. For Alvin, he could do this and so much more.

Thankfully, Jasper seemed to know where he was going. He put a hand on Roman's back and guided him down the hallway, and since Roman didn't have to worry about where he was going, it allowed him to look around.

There was more than one cell door open. What did that mean?

"There's Thomas," Jasper said.

The badger alpha stood next to an open door, talking to a man in a guard's uniform and another man in a suit. Roman had no idea who they were, and he didn't care. He only cared about Alvin.

He rushed forward, hoping against all odds that Alvin would be there. Thomas looked alarmed when he saw him barreling toward him, and he had to put out his hands so that Roman wouldn't slam into him.

"What happened to you?" he asked, his gaze going to the butterfly bandages on Roman's forehead.

"Harvey shot me. Where's Alvin?"

"We don't know. Silas isn't the only prisoner who escaped. We have different situations happening all over the jail. One of the prisoners took two guards hostage, but most of the people who got free seem to have escaped."

"Who's here?" Jasper asked.

"Morris is dealing with the hostage situation. Luther and his team are here, but Josiah stayed home. The fox alpha is also around. He and some of his people are looking for the escapees. More people are coming. I don't think we'll find Silas, though. He's a smart man, so he'd have gotten out of here as soon as he could."

Jasper nodded. "He's not who I'm worried about."

"You should be."

Jasper shrugged. "I'll have plenty of time to worry about him once this is over. Harvey took Alvin and shot Roman. It's a miracle he's alive. He heard Harvey mention Alvin taking the blame for what's happening, and we want to make sure none of the guards will hurt him."

"We'll do our best, but as of now, no one has reported him being anywhere. I'm sorry, Roman."

Roman nodded. There was nothing Thomas could do about it. Everyone was working to get the prisoners back into their cells and help the people who'd been wounded, and Roman should be doing the same. No matter how worried he was about Alvin, he was a healer, and his first duty was to help anyone wounded. He didn't have his bag with him, but he was sure the jail had an infirmary or something similar.

"I can help with whoever's been hurt as long as I have supplies," he said.

Thomas gestured at the two men standing with him. "This is Seth Wilson. He's the man in charge of this place."

"I can take you to the infirmary," the man said. "Or I can have someone bring you a kit."

"The second option, please. I won't know how badly people are hurt, and I don't want to move them before I can ascertain it."

The man nodded and turned to the guard to give him an order. The guard quickly left, and for a moment, Roman felt lost.

He needed to find Alvin, but how could he? His job was to help people, and there were plenty who needed him. From where he was, he could see a wounded guard down the hall-way. The man was sitting up and talking, so he was probably all right, but Roman would have to check him. That meant he couldn't focus on Alvin.

Jasper squeezed Roman's shoulder. "I'll look for him while you're busy."

"Thank you. I just hate that I don't know what Harvey and Silas did to him."

"I do, too. But they probably wouldn't have hurt him if they wanted him to take the blame for what happened here. We need to keep that in mind."

Roman nodded. Jasper was right, but how could he focus on that while he didn't know what had happened to Alvin?

Knowing him and how stubborn he was, he'd probably tried to escape as soon as he had the opportunity to do so. What if Harvey had killed him to stop him from leaving? Hell, Alvin might even have tried to escape before they got here. He could be dead somewhere in the forest, and Roman would never find him.

Someone came running toward them, and Roman shook himself out of his thoughts. He needed to focus on what he could do, and at the moment, that was helping the people around him. He could break down once these people were taken care of.

If anything had happened to Alvin, he *would* break down. Alvin had wormed his way under Roman's skin and into his heart, and there would be no dislodging him. If something had happened to him, it would destroy Roman, and he didn't know if he could deal with more grief than he'd already had to deal with lately.

But that was a problem for Roman of the future. Roman of the present had a job to do, and he'd do it.

Chapter Fifteen

A lvin didn't know how long he stayed in the cell. Eventually, someone shut down the alarm, which was a relief for his ears. They continued ringing for a while after that, but it was a discomfort Alvin could deal with. It meant he wasn't dead.

The problem was that now that he was mostly safe, he had nothing to do. All of his thoughts were focused on Roman and on whether or not he'd made it, and not knowing the answer to that was maddening. Was Roman all right? Had he woken up yet?

Alvin wouldn't find out until he was allowed out of the cell.

For a while, he paced, but his leg started to ache. He almost forced himself to continue, but hurting himself even more wouldn't help anyone. When they saw each other again, Roman would scold Alvin for doing it, and Alvin didn't want that, so he sat on the bed that was against one of the walls.

He could hear voices outside but didn't know what they were saying. People kept walking in front of the cell, and he'd initially called out but quickly stopped. These people didn't care about him or that he was locked up even though he wasn't involved. They were probably still focused on recapturing the prisoners and helping whoever had been hurt during this mess. To them, he was just another prisoner.

But his place wasn't here. It was in skunk territory with Roman.

When the lock clicked open, Alvin jumped to his feet. He

wanted to rush forward, but he knew better. Whoever was coming in would probably think he was trying to escape, and he needed these people to believe he was on their side.

He stayed where he was. He watched as a man and a woman walked into the room, frowning at the way they were dressed. They wore uniforms, but it wasn't the jail guards' uniform. It didn't look like what the council guards wore, either.

"Your name?" the man asked.

"Alvin. Please, I need to talk to someone. My boyfriend was shot when I was dragged here, and I need to know if he's okay."

The two looked at each other. "What do you mean your boyfriend was shot? This happened before you were locked up?" the woman asked.

"I'm not a prisoner here. I was brought here to take the blame for letting the former skunk alpha out, but I had nothing to do with it. You have to believe me. Until a few hours ago, I was in skunk territory. Call Jasper or his alpha mate, Dean. They'll be able to tell you all about it."

The guards looked surprised. "You know Dean?" the man asked.

Alvin tried not to hope too hard. "I do. He'll tell you who I am if you talk to him."

Alvin doubted Jasper would have let Dean come to the jail after finding out his father had been freed, but if these people knew Dean, they could call him. They might trust him more than they trusted Jasper. Alvin had no way to know for sure, but the fact that they wore different uniforms made him wonder if they were shifters. Dean had mentioned that he'd moved into the forest with his family and a team of humans he used to work with, and maybe that was who these two people were.

The woman looked at the man, who nodded. "Go in the

hallway and call him."

The woman obeyed, leaving Alvin alone with the man. They stared at each other for a while, and Alvin wondered if he needed to do or say something. Was there a way for him to convince this guy that he was on the right side?

"My name is Luther," the man eventually said.

"Alvin."

Luther looked surprised. "The human?"

He made it sound like Alvin was famous, although Alvin suspected that if he was, it was for all the wrong reasons. "I'm human, yes."

"I've heard about you from Josiah, my partner. He's the coyote alpha."

Alvin tried to think of what he knew about Josiah. Roman had been telling him a lot about the people who lived in the forest, especially the people he liked. Josiah was one of those people. Roman had mentioned he was pregnant and that he was dating a human.

"If you had nothing to do with any of this, you don't have to worry. I'll make sure you make it out of this cell," Luther added.

If Luther had been a shifter, Alvin wouldn't have believed him. It would be too easy for the council or an alpha to force Alvin to stay here. Jasper and Roman would argue, but that didn't mean they would win.

But Luther was human. He didn't answer to the council, and while he did have to answer to his alpha, that alpha was his partner. Knowing that made Alvin feel better, but he still had no idea what had happened to Roman. "Thank you. Do you know if Jasper is here? Or maybe Dean?"

"I haven't seen either of them."

"I just need to know what happened to my boyfriend. He was shot when I was kidnapped, and he was unconscious the last time I saw him." Alvin was repeating himself, but he couldn't think of anything else. "I promise I'm not the enemy."

Luther grimaced. "I can see why you're anxious."

The cell door opened, and the woman peeked in. "I have Dean on the phone."

Luther nodded. "What did he say?"

"He wants to talk to you."

Luther held out his hand, and the woman put the phone into it. Luther paused, then touched the screen. "Dean?" he asked.

"Luther. Alvin is one of ours." Dean's voice was loud in the cell.

Alvin had known Dean would be on his side, but hearing it felt good. Part of him had wondered if maybe Dean and Jasper would decide it was better if they got rid of him. It would certainly be easier for the surfeit.

"Can you tell me about him?" Luther asked.

"He's that human we talked about, the one who snuck in through the hole in the fence. He's harmless and a surfeit member. The old beta kidnapped him."

"Dean," Alvin blurted out. He had to guess that Luther had put the call on speaker because he'd wanted Alvin to be able to participate. "Do you know what happened to Roman? Is he all right?"

"It's good to hear your voice," Dean said. "And yes, he's fine. He's in the same building as you, caring for the wounded guards."

Alvin's legs went weak, and he had to sit down. Luckily for him, the bed wasn't far. He slumped onto it and tried to breathe, but it was hard.

Roman was all right. Even though Harvey had shot him, he'd survived and was already working.

Alvin wasn't surprised. That was exactly like Roman, and he was sure that if everyone had been all right, Roman would have been rushing down the hallways calling his name.

Alvin wasn't offended by the fact that his boyfriend wasn't there trying to save him. Roman took his job as a healer seriously. If people were wounded, he needed to be with them.

"We'll let him out of the cell and try to find Jasper," Luther said. "I'll make sure no one locks him up again. I don't know what happened. The fox alpha told us a prisoner insisted on talking to Jasper, but he didn't go into details."

"It's fine," Dean told Luther. "As long as Alvin is okay, everything's fine."

"Harvey didn't hurt me," Alvin said. "He wanted me to take the blame for what happened with Silas, but I managed to run away. I found two guards, but I understand why they couldn't trust me. I just want out of the cell and to make sure Roman is okay."

"You don't have to worry about any of that. You're free," Luther told Alvin.

Alvin hoped he was right. He might be free now, but he still didn't know what would happen with the council.

It wasn't something he needed to worry about now, though. Right now, he only wanted to find Roman, reassure him that he was all right, and reassure himself that Roman wasn't in pain. Roman would work even if he was wounded, but it was time for Alvin to take care of him the way he'd taken care of Alvin.

Alvin wouldn't have it any other way.

"You can take her to the infirmary," Roman said, looking up.

The guard he'd been talking to nodded and helped the woman Roman had been treating to her feet. Roman watched them for a second, just to be sure. She had a wound in her thigh, but it should heal without trouble. She'd be able to come back to work soon.

He was done treating the guards who'd been hurt when the prisoners had escaped. There were still a few with scratches and bruises, but they didn't need immediate help, which was a good thing because Roman was exhausted. He wouldn't leave until he was sure everyone was cared for, but he could breathe.

But not before he found Alvin.

Roman straightened and stretched his back. He wanted nothing more than to go to bed, slip under the sheets, and stay there for the next couple of days, but he wasn't done yet.

He turned to Jasper, who was standing at the edge of the room and quietly talking with Thomas. "Is there anyone else I need to see?"

Jasper shook his head. "I don't think so. The infirmary doctors have everything in hand."

Roman hadn't been working alone. As soon as the building had been secured, the two doctors who worked here had left the infirmary. They'd been hiding, which was a good thing because it meant no one had hurt them, so they were able to help everyone who needed it. The wounded people were mostly guards, although a few prisoners had been hurt after they'd gotten into fights or tried to escape.

Knowing he was off the hook meant Roman could focus on Alvin.

Where was he? Roman hadn't seen him, but he'd been told Alvin was in the building. What did that mean? Roman didn't even know if he was hurt. Jasper had reassured him that everything was fine, but Roman wouldn't truly believe it until Alvin was in front of him. He trusted Jasper, but the situation was too much of a mess.

The sound of a door opening made Roman turn. He was ready to help if someone else needed him. It was getting late, but it wouldn't stop him from doing his job.

A woman walked in, quickly followed by two men.

One of them was Alvin.

Roman dropped everything and rushed forward, almost falling on his face. The woman looked alarmed, but Alvin pushed past her, opening his arms. Roman threw himself against him, crying out when his body made contact with Alvin.

"What happened to you?" he asked. "Where were you?"

"I'm here, and I'm fine," Alvin promised. "I'm sorry I made you worry."

Roman wanted to shake him, but none of this had been Alvin's fault. Whatever had happened rested on Silas's and Harvey's shoulders. They'd have to pay for it, but that wasn't something Roman would be involved with. He didn't want to be.

Roman leaned back to look at his boyfriend. He needed to make sure Alvin was fine now that he knew that he was safe, and he had to resist the urge to drag him toward the closest seat and force him to sit down.

"How's your leg?" he asked, relieved to see that Alvin didn't have any visible wounds.

Alvin grimaced. "It aches a bit, but it's nothing I can't deal with. They didn't hurt me. No one did."

That seemed to be true. Roman didn't think he would fully believe it until he got Alvin naked and checked every inch of his body, but for now, this was good enough. "Where were you?" he asked, not releasing Alvin. He didn't think he'd be able to let go for a while.

"I was locked up in a cell."

Roman sucked in a breath. "They locked you up?"

The man who'd walked in with Alvin cleared his throat, getting Roman's attention. Roman recognized him now that he was looking at him, and he had to resist the urge to punch his friend Josiah's boyfriend.

Luther grimaced. "The fox alpha locked him up. He

warned me that two of his people had found a human running around the facility. They didn't know who he was, but
they'd seen him with Harvey and Silas, so they didn't trust
him. It's why the alpha asked me and Miriam to look into it."

"Why did anyone think it was a good idea to lock him up?
It's clear he wasn't involved in any of this."

Luther raised his hands. "Everyone did their job. He's free
to go now, of course."

"He's right," Alvin said gently. "I know you were scared,
and I was, too. He didn't know what had happened to you. I
understand why they felt the need to lock me up, though, and
I don't hold it against them. They did what they had to in order to feel safe, and I can't blame them for that."

Roman thought that he *could* blame them for it and that if
he ever saw the fox alpha, he'd be sure to tell him that, but
Alvin wasn't wrong. He was healthy and free. There was no
reason for them to linger here.

Roman turned to Jasper. "I'm done here. I want to go
home."

"I'll take both of you. Or do you need us to stay?" he asked,
turning to Thomas.

Thomas shook his head. "I don't think there's anything anyone can do beyond what we've already done. The hostages
are free, and while we're still missing some prisoners, it's getting late. You're not involved with the recovery of the people
who escaped, so you should go home. Be careful, though.
Harvey and Silas are out there, and we both know they'll be
coming for you."

They would, and Roman was worried. What would they
do? Roman knew them well enough to be sure they'd try to
get revenge on Jasper. Harvey felt like Jasper had taken something that wasn't his by becoming the alpha, and he'd never
been the alpha to begin with. There was no way Silas would
stand back and allow his son to guide the surfeit now that he

was free. They'd try something, but probably not tonight, which meant Roman and Alvin might be able to rest.

They'd get ready to fight tomorrow. Tonight, Roman wanted to relax and act as if everything was perfectly all right in his world.

"I already called Dean and warned him," Jasper told Thomas. "He talked to the guards so they know to be careful. I doubt I'll be able to get much sleep until my father and Harvey are both apprehended, but this is good enough for now."

Thomas looked like he disagreed. "Would you be offended if I asked some of my guards to come with you? I don't want you to believe I think you're unable to protect yourself and your people or that I'm trying to invade your territory. I know Silas, maybe better than you do. You've always seen him as a father, but I've worked with him for years. He's ruthless, and now that he's free, he'll come for you. I'm sure your guards are well-trained, but he was their alpha for decades. No matter how much they respect you and how frightened they are of him, his presence might be enough for them to give in."

"I'd be happy to have your guards in my territory," Jasper said.

Roman was relieved. He wouldn't have been surprised if Jasper had said no. Most alphas would have. It could feel like Thomas was trying to take over the surfeit, and if he'd been anyone else, it might have been what he was trying to do.

But not Thomas. He was a good man, and Roman believed he just wanted to help. He didn't want Silas to take over the surfeit again any more than Jasper did, and he'd do what he could to help ensure it didn't happen.

It took a while longer for everything to be in place, but eventually, Roman and Alvin finally followed Jasper out of the building. Roman felt like he might fall asleep at any moment, but first, he wanted to check Alvin and make sure he wasn't hurt. He wanted to ask Alvin what had happened with

Harvey, but he felt it wasn't a good idea. Alvin probably didn't want to think about it any longer today.

"If it's all right with you, I'll come over tomorrow to talk," Jasper said as he drove them home.

"I'm fine with that," Alvin told him. "I'm not surprised you want to talk, but thank you for waiting."

"Alvin is coming home with me, so you don't have to drive him to the cabin," Roman said. He'd been rude by interrupting them, but he didn't care. He wasn't letting Alvin out of his sight ever again if he had anything to say about it.

"I expected that," Jasper said with a smile. "We're not done with the council and Foley, but I understand why you want Alvin close. We'll have to be careful, but I don't think it's going to be a problem."

Roman wasn't sure about that, but he was done hiding. He was done allowing people to treat Alvin like he'd done something wrong when he hadn't.

Alvin's place was with Roman, in his home and his heart. Roman didn't care what anyone had to say about that, and he'd fight Foley or anyone else who threatened Alvin.

Alvin wasn't the enemy, and it was time people started to accept that.

EPILOGUE

Things had been quiet, possibly too quiet.

Alvin had expected Foley and his allies to barge into skunk territory again after what had happened at the jail, but they hadn't. He hadn't seen them in a while, but he wondered if he would today.

He glanced sideways at Roman, who was sitting next to him. He appeared calm and collected, which was the opposite of how Alvin felt.

Alvin had been shielded from most of what was happening outside of skunk territory since Roman had found him under the tree, but that was over now. He'd had to leave his home today because he was meeting with the council.

He swallowed and looked at the massive double doors in front of him. What would they decide? There was no way to know before he saw them, but he was nervous. Everyone knew what had happened at the jail by now. They knew that Silas was gone and that Alvin had been there, so Alvin wouldn't be surprised if the council had questions for him or if they suspected he'd been involved. No matter how many times he swore he hadn't been, there would always be someone who didn't believe him. As long as the right people did, he didn't care.

The problem was that the council held Alvin's future in their hands.

He was a surfeit member, so he had no doubt that Jasper would stand up for him if the council decided to kick him out. He'd do it because Alvin was one of his people, but also because Alvin was a friend.

But Alvin didn't want Jasper to be in trouble, which was what would happen if he stood up to the council. If they decided to kick Alvin out, he wouldn't have to deal with them again once he was out of the forest, but Jasper would. The council could create countless problems for the surfeit, and Alvin didn't feel it would be worth it.

He wasn't sure *he* was worth it.

A hand landed on his knee, startling him. He turned to see that Roman was frowning at him, and he quickly tried to reassure his boyfriend. "I'm sure everything will be all right."

Roman squeezed Alvin's knee. "I believe that, but I'm not sure you do. You look worried."

Alvin sighed. "That's because I am. No matter what I think will happen, there's a chance that things will go sideways."

Jasper, who was standing next to the bench on which Alvin and Roman were sitting, leaned closer. "Whatever happens, I'll stand by your side."

Alvin opened his mouth to tell him that was what he was afraid of, but one of the doors in front of them opened. It quickly closed again after a woman stepped out, but Alvin had enough time to see a long table with people gathered around it.

This was it. He was about to meet the council.

The woman who'd opened the door nodded at him. "They're ready for you."

Alvin wanted to tell her that *he* wasn't ready for *them*, but instead, he got to his feet and squared his shoulders.

Whatever happened in that room, he'd fight to be able to stay. Even if he was dragged back to the edge of the forest, he'd find a way to return. This was his home now, and he wouldn't allow anyone to kick him out, not even the council.

Roman slipped his hand into Alvin's and linked their fingers together. They followed Jasper to the door, and even though Jasper behaved as if he didn't have a care in the world, Alvin could see he was worried.

Jasper opened the door and stepped aside to let Alvin and Roman in, then followed them. The door closed behind Jasper.

Alvin looked around, wondering what it was like to have the power the council members had. With one decision, they could ruin the lives of at least two people. If they didn't allow Alvin to stay, he didn't know what would happen to him and Roman. As much as they wanted to be together, it might not be possible, and Alvin had no idea how to deal with that.

One step at a time, he supposed.

"You can sit," one of the women at the table said.

Roman had told Alvin that the council was made up of one representative for every shifter group in the forest. When everyone was there, there were thirteen council members at the table. Alvin could see several empty seats, so he knew they hadn't all come.

Ronald was there. Alvin resisted the urge to glare at him, instead focusing on the woman who'd told him to sit. He didn't know her, but she was smiling, which he hoped meant she was on his side.

He sat down. Roman took the seat next to him, but Jasper remained standing behind them, almost as if he was protecting them. Maybe in his mind, he was. Alvin doubted the council would attack him, but that didn't mean they couldn't hurt him.

"The first thing we wish to do is apologize," the woman said, startling Alvin.

"Apologize?"

"We reviewed the CCTV from the day of the escape and talked to the guard who let Harvey in. We know you had nothing to do with what happened, and I'm sorry we treated you as if you were guilty." She glanced toward Ronald, who looked like he'd eaten a lemon.

Alvin suspected that Ronald had tried to push everyone into making him leave, but it looked like he hadn't succeeded. Alvin told himself not to hope, but it was hard. "Thank you, ma'am."

"Please, call me Marjory."

Alvin liked Marjory. He had no idea who she represented, but he wasn't sure it mattered. She clearly was on his side since she was apologizing.

A man cleared his throat. Alvin turned to look at him, wondering who he was. He didn't have to wonder very long. "My name is Christopher, and I'm the opossum representative on the council. We looked into your claim that you had opossum shifters in your family tree and can confirm it. We can also confirm that your ancestors came from this area. As far as we're concerned, you have every right to be here. I'd offer you a place with the opossums, but I doubt you'll accept, which is perfectly fine. My alpha and I want you to know that you'll always be welcome with us, though."

Alvin's heart raced. Was Christopher saying what he thought he was saying? "Does this mean I'm allowed to stay?"

Christopher smiled. "You are. We agreed that while you entered the forest in an unconventional way, you didn't do anything wrong. We don't have a law that says that what you did was breaking and entering, just like we don't have a law that says humans can't live here. Some people might feel differently, but this is your home, and how you entered it doesn't matter. Welcome to Allegheny Forest, Alvin."

Alvin wasn't going to cry in front of these people. He didn't want to show them how important this was to him, although they could probably tell. Ronald was there, and there was no way Alvin would give him that. His feelings were reserved for people who cared about him.

"Thank you," he said in a trembling voice.

There was nothing else to say. Alvin was interested in Christopher and in finding out more about his ancestors, but it wasn't something he wanted to deal with now. He just wanted to go home with the certainty that he actually belonged. Roman's house already felt like home, but now, it truly would be. Alvin would never have to leave.

For so long, he'd searched for a place where he'd belong. He'd finally found it. He'd finally been able to convince these people that he wasn't the enemy.

But Harvey and Silas were. They were still out there, and Alvin had no doubt they would become a problem soon. He was ready to fight for the people he loved and his new family.

He might only be human, but he wouldn't allow anyone to take his dream away.

ABOUT THE AUTHOR

Catherine is the creator of several series, most of them paranormal, including the Whitedell Pride Series and the Gillham Pack Series. While she graduated in translation, she decided to go the writer's way because it was more fun to create her own stories and characters.

She's been living in Italy for more than twenty years, but she's a daughter of the North—Belgium to be precise—and she misses it so much that she's already planning to move back.

She loves pizza—probably too much—her son, her pets, and of course, books. She sneaks some reading time into her schedule every time she has five minutes free from writing, demands from her various pets and son, and lastly, housework.

Connect with her:

lievens.catherine@gmail.com
BookBub: https://www.bookbub.com/authors/catherine-lievens
Website: https://authorcatherinelievens.com/
Facebook: https://www.facebook.com/catherine.lievens.9
Facebook Group: https://www.facebook.com/groups/411788002341528/
Twitter: https://twitter.com/authorCLievens

Newsletter: http://eepurl.com/c-uvKn